Aftermath Series Book Two

# AFTERMATH OF A PARTY

V K McGivney

Authors Reach
www.authorsreach.co.uk

ISBN: 978-1-9160626-7-2

My sincere thanks to Beta readers Shani Struthers and Corinna Edwards-Colledge; to Diane Stewart for her helpful comments, and to Gina Dickerson for her cover design and invaluable help with formatting and production.

# Prologue

'Stella' I hear myself screaming. She's lying on the kitchen floor and a deep red stain is spreading through her lovely white dress. The man standing over her turns and comes towards me. There's a kind of humming in my ears. Everything goes black.

# Chapter 1

'Hanna, Miss Walker, wake up!'

Compelled to obey, I force myself into consciousness, open my eyes but quickly close them again as the light is too bright and there's a throbbing pain in my skull. There seems to be a tight band around my head and a kind of mask over my nose and mouth that's emitting cool air.

Something is squeezing the top of my left arm; it gets tighter and tighter then abruptly loosens.

'Wake up, Hanna!' The voice is insistent. 'Wake up!'

I open my eyes again and try to clear my sight. The lids feel weighted but I can make out the blurry face of a woman leaning over me. I hear clanks and bangs and a telephone ringing in the distance.

The woman removes the mask from my nose and mouth. 'All over, dear.'

'What's all over?' My voice comes out as a faint croak. 'Where am I?'

She smiles at me. 'In hospital, dear.'

'Hospital?' I'm bewildered. 'What am I doing here? It's cold.'

She pulls a thin blanket over me. 'Better now?'

'My head hurts.'

'It will hurt for a while.' She reaches across and gently

adjusts what I realise is a bandage attached to my head and covering half of my ears. 'You've been in Intensive Care. You've had emergency surgery.'

'Surgery?' I have difficulty grasping what she means. 'What surgery?'

'Neurosurgery, to reduce the pressure on your brain, control the bleeding and remove any blood clots.'

I gasp with shock. 'Blood clots? What's happened? Have I been in an accident?'

But she has already moved away and I hear her speaking to someone else. I catch a few words about complications.

My eyes close again. All I want to do is abandon myself to sleep.

\* \* \*

Voices. Footsteps.

I remember I'm in a hospital. Why am I here? How long have I been here?

Someone takes my temperature then my blood pressure. A man shines a light in my eyes and asks me questions about my vision.

'It's blurry,' I tell him.

He writes a note on a chart.

A nurse hands me some pills and a glass of water. I swallow the pills. My throat feels sore. My head drops back on the pillow.

\* \* \*

Daylight.

A nurse helps me sit up. Despite the fuzziness of my

vision, I see that I'm in a small room. Mine is the only bed. It feels warm in here, stuffy, and I can smell something like disinfectant.

My head hurts.

I discover I'm hooked up to a heart monitor and there's a drip in the back of my left hand. It feels sore.

A woman comes in and sits down next to my bed. She tells me she's a consultant neurologist and that I'm in a neurological high dependency unit. 'You're here because you have a head injury which has affected your brain. It's called Traumatic Brain Injury; "TBI" for short.'

I feel totally bewildered. 'Why? Have I been in an accident?'

'We think the injury was caused by something heavy– a blunt instrument – which has resulted in a blunt force trauma to your skull.'

'How? Did I fall? Was I knocked down?'

She shakes her head. 'I don't know how it happened'

'How long have I been here?'

'Three days.'

'*Three days*?' Have I lost three whole days of my life?

'You were put in an induced coma and you've had surgery to remove a haematoma and release some of the pressure in your skull.'

'What?' The information is almost impossible to take in. 'Am I ...will I ... recover?'

'We hope so, but TBI can affect a person's cognitive skills and mental processes. Fortunately your speech doesn't seem to be badly affected but you must alert a nurse immediately if it becomes slurred or if you experience any of the following....' She cites a terrifyingly long list of potential symptoms.

'Oh God!'

'Try not to worry. You're being well looked after. You'll be closely monitored and you've been put on AEDs.'

'What are they?'

'Anti seizure drugs.'

If she thinks this is reassuring, she's mistaken.

After the consultant leaves, the nurse returns to my bedside. She's smiling. 'Your sister, Mrs Fry is here. We found your next-of-kin details and called her. She's been here for two days, waiting to see how you are.'

The nurse's face is replaced by the anxious one of my sister Penny. She peers down at me. 'Thank God,' she breathes. 'I've been so worried. Whatever happened to you, Hanna?'

'I don't know,' I mumble. 'I've no idea.'

She takes hold of my hand. 'How are you feeling now?'

'Rough.' I tentatively touch the side of my head.

'At least you're out of intensive care. They say you'll have to go through various tests but there's a good chance you'll recover.'

'Is there?' I feel too tired to even think about it.

She sits with me for a while but I'm not up to making conversation. Finally she stands and squeezes my hand. 'I hate to leave you so soon but I really need to go home this evening. John's been looking after the children while I've been here.' She plants a kiss on my cheek. 'I'll call the hospital every day to check on how you are and I'll come back as soon as I can.'

'Yes, thank you.' My eyes are already shutting.

# Chapter 2

'Are you awake, Hanna? A gentleman has been waiting to speak to you.'

Through my blurred vision, I make out the outline of a thickset man standing next to a nurse at the foot of my bed.

'Do you feel well enough to talk, Ms Walker?' he asks. 'The doctor said I can have a few minutes.'

I squeeze my eyes to try and clear my sight and stare at him. Who is he?

'What do you want to talk to me about?' My voice is still a faint croak.

'I'm Detective Inspector Forrester.' The man shows me his ID but I can't read the writing on it. 'May I call you Hanna?' he asks.

'Yes.'

'Thank you. If you feel up to it, Hanna, I'd like to ask you a few questions about what happened.'

'Happened?' I struggle to sit up. The nurse cranks up the bed and puts a pillow behind my head before moving away. I can hear footsteps in the corridor outside the room.

'Can you tell me what happened at the party?' The man draws a chair up to the side of my bed and sits down. He's middle-aged with very thick black eyebrows, pouches under his eyes and deep grooves on each side of his mouth.

'Party? What party?' It's very warm, almost stifling, in the room, and I take a sip of water from the glass on the locker beside my bed. My hand trembles with the effort.

'Your friend Stella's birthday party. You were there. Do you remember going to the party, Hanna?' He waits in silence while I try to clear the fog from my mind.

I feel totally disoriented; wonder what he's talking about. 'I don't remember what happened before I woke up here,' I tell him. 'They say I have traumatic amnesia.'

'I know. We think someone must have hit you on the head with something – a weapon or a heavy object.'

I start with shock. 'What do you mean someone hit me? Who? Why would anyone hit me on the head?'

'That's what we're trying to find out,' he says gently.

'But how? Why--?'

A trolley stops at the door of my room and a woman comes in. 'Tea, dear?' she asks me.

'Yes, please.' I'm grateful for the interruption. It gives me more time to absorb the alarming information I've just received.

'Milk? Sugar?'

The woman pours me a cup of tea and puts it on the locker beside my bed. I pick it up and take a sip but it's so hot and my throat so sore that I swallow the liquid with difficulty.

The detective resumes as soon as the woman has left the room. 'I'm sorry to say you were attacked at your friend's flat.'

'Why?' My hand is shaking so much that I need to replace the cup on the locker before tea spills onto the bed.

'We're not sure but we think it was probably because you witnessed something.'

'What? What am I supposed to have witnessed?'

He doesn't answer my question and instead asks another of his own. 'Can you recall what happened at the party, Hanna?'

'What party?' Why is he pestering me with these questions? My head hurts and I want to sleep.

'Your friend, Stella Whitmore's birthday party; it was her fortieth.' He articulates slowly and clearly as though I'm deaf or have learning difficulties. 'Do you remember going to it? She held it in her flat. You were there. You were one of the guests.'

'I'm sorry. I don't know what you're talking about?' I can hear the sound of trolleys being wheeled along the corridor.

'You were there, at Stella's party,' the detective repeats. 'Don't you remember being at the party, Hanna?'

'No, I don't remember anything.'

My head is throbbing and my brain seems to be encased in cotton wool. I desperately want to go back to sleep but he's looking at me expectantly, obviously waiting for me to say something more.

'Please try to remember. It was Stella's party. You were there.'

I strain to think but feel so sluggish that the effort exhausts me.

'The party... Stella's party,' he repeats. 'Try to remember.'

The mist begins to clear.

I'm looking at myself in a full-length mirror and hating what I see – nose too long, eyes too small, hair too lank, dress too tight, revealing bulges in places where bulges shouldn't be. I don't want to go. Will anyone speak to me? Normally I avoid such occasions but I promised Stella I'd go as it's her fortieth and I can't think of an excuse that will sound plausible or that she'll accept. I know exactly what it will be like: it'll be dominated by Stella's "inner circle" – good-looking, beautifully dressed people, totally at ease and full of confidence. They'll be clustered in impenetrable groups that always seem to be dominated by one of those individuals with that indefinable "something" – charisma or magnetism – that seems to blind others to the fact that their conversation is mainly about themselves.

I'll try all the social tricks supposed to make one feel at ease – introduce myself to people, smile a lot, ask them questions about themselves, and make a show of listening, but I know their gaze will rapidly swivel away in search of someone more interesting, and then I'll find myself standing on my own like a wallflower at an old-fashioned dance, trying to appear relaxed and uncaring; gulping wine too fast...

I have a sudden image of Stella, dazzling in a figure-hugging white dress. She's smiling and holding a champagne glass in her hand.

I give a convulsive start. 'Stella!'

'Yes?' The detective leans towards me eagerly. 'Have you remembered something, Hanna?'

I gasp for I *have* remembered something: Blood! Blood on the floor; blood seeping through Stella's white dress ...

The scene is frozen, like a stilled film frame.

'Is Stella OK?' I whisper.

'Do you know any reason why she wouldn't be OK?' he asks sharply.

'The dress.'

'What dress?'

'Hers, Stella's – her white dress. There's blood on it.'

The detective takes out a notebook and pen. 'Do you know *how* the blood got on her dress, Hanna? Take your time.'

But the vision has already dissipated. 'No, I'm too tired.'

He waits for a moment, then as I remain silent, says, 'Something happened in the kitchen of Stella's flat after her birthday party had finished. We know that most of the guests had left by 12.30. You were still there at the time. You were still in the flat after the other guests had gone.'

'I can't have been,' I mutter. 'I always leave parties early.'

'Not on this occasion,' he says gently. 'You stayed on after the other guests had left and we estimate that what happened to you would have been shortly afterwards.'

'How do you know that?'

'We know you were still there because you were found in the kitchen with Stella.'

I'm bewildered. 'What do you mean, "found"?'

He shakes his head slightly but doesn't explain.

Fatigue envelops me like a thick blanket and I suddenly feel sick.

The detective is shooed away by a nurse.

# Chapter 3

He returns the next day with another police officer, a youngish woman who's introduced to me as DS Something, but I don't catch her name. They both pull up chairs and sit beside my bed.

After expressing the hope that I'm feeling a little better, DI Forrester asks, 'Have you remembered what happened before you were brought here, Hanna?'

'No.'

'Nothing at all?'

'Nothing.' I feel inexplicably guilty.

He nods in a resigned sort of way. 'Well hopefully something will come back to you when you begin to feel better.'

'Maybe.'

'I'm sorry to bother you with all these questions,' he says, 'but they're very important. Can you recall whether anyone else stayed on in Stella's flat after the other guests had left? Did anyone who *wasn't* a guest at the party turn up after it had finished?'

'I don't know. I told you I can't remember anything about the party or how I got here.' My voice comes out as a childish wail. Tears fill my eyes and threaten to spill down my cheeks.

The female officer leans towards me. She has large, pale blue eyes. 'Don't distress yourself, Hanna. Just take your time. Would you like some water?'

'Yes, please.'

She hands me the glass from my locker and I take a sip.

'Maybe you can remember something that happened *before* the party, Hanna,' DI Forrester continues. 'Was Stella upset for any reason?'

'I don't know. I don't remember.'

'Do you know whether she'd quarrelled with anyone? Do you recall her having any arguments in the period leading up to the party?'

'No.' My mind wanders and I gaze, fascinated, at the man's amazingly bushy black eyebrows. They seem to have a life of their own. Does he ever trim them? Why are they so much darker than the hair on his head? I realise he's still speaking to me. His voice seems far away and I make an effort to concentrate on what he's saying.

'Such a beautiful woman might have aroused resentment in some quarters, from a spurned admirer perhaps, or envy from a jealous love rival. Can you think of anyone who might have had a grudge against her?'

'I'm sorry, I can't think of anyone offhand.' I wish they would go away and leave me alone.

The female officer seems to understand my feelings. She smiles at me. 'Just say if you want to take a break, Hanna.'

There's a brief silence, then the detective says, 'Well let's get back to the party. Can you remember anything about it at all, Hanna?

'No.'

'Not even the smallest detail?'

'I've been trying,' I tell him resentfully.

Long moments pass.

Suddenly a scene begins to unfold behind my eyelids: it's like watching something on a screen, but the picture's dark and indistinct. I see myself entering Stella's kitchen. She's lying on the floor and there's a man with his back to me leaning over her. Who is he? He turns and comes towards me, then everything goes black.

With difficulty I drag myself back into the present. 'Stella – she's lying on the floor, and there's someone standing over her; a man.'

'What man?' DI Forrester asks sharply. 'Who is it?'

'I don't know.' The scene, which lasted less than a second, has evaporated.

'Describe it again, exactly what you remembered.' His tone is urgent.

'It may not have been a memory,' I falter. 'It was more like a dream...a nightmare.'

'What did the man look like?'

'I don't know. He had his back to me.'

'Try to think. Was he tall?'

'I don't know.'

'What was he wearing? What colour was his hair?'

'I d-don't know. I'm not even sure what I saw was real; it could have been my imagination.'

'But it could have been a flashback of what actually happened, which suggests you may have seen what that person did to Stella.'

Alarm bells begin to jangle in my head. 'What do you mean, *did* to Stella? Is Stella OK?'

He's silent for a moment then regards me steadily and says very quietly, 'I'm afraid Stella's dead, Hanna.'

'*Dead*?' I gaze at him and start to tremble. 'Dead?'

'I'm afraid so.'

'That's not possible.'

'I'm sorry but it's true; Stella's dead.'

'She can't be.'

The woman officer leans across the bed and grips one of my hands.

'I'm sorry,' the detective repeats. 'She was murdered that night, after the party. You and Stella were both found on the kitchen floor. She was dead and you were badly injured. That's why you're here.'

I clutch convulsively at the sheet with my free hand as a wave of nausea engulfs me. 'Who...? How? How was she...?'

He hesitates for a moment and glances at his colleague. 'Stella was stabbed. We don't yet know who by.' He doesn't go into any more detail.

The ceiling seems to be falling in; darkness is closing in on me. I fall back on the pillow.

# Chapter 4

I can't believe that Stella's dead; that she no longer exists. I feel abandoned.

Stella has always been part of my life. We've known each other forever. We used to live in the same street. We spent most of our childhood and teenage years together. At school, we were the classic female duo – the pretty one and the plain one: Stella with her dark blue eyes and blond, almost white, hair; vivacious and fun-loving, always in demand; me: overweight, mousy-haired and socially awkward, forever trailing in the brilliance of her wake, the contrast between us throwing her beauty into even sharper relief. I had other friends, but Stella, whom I adored, always took precedence.

All the girls envied Stella and all the boys lusted after her. If one of them ever paid any attention to me, it was only because he hoped I'd act as a conduit to her. Except for JC, of course. (John Christopher Sims was always known as JC because there was another John in the class). For reasons I could never understand, he always seemed to prefer me to Stella, but although JC was pleasant enough, I was never attracted to him, at least, not "in that way". He once told me he thought Stella wasn't a nice person; he found her selfish and self-regarding. Stella *was* self-absorbed, but I didn't care because I loved her. She soaked up admiration like a sponge, accepting the homage to her beauty as her due, as I would have done had I been similarly blessed. Unlike the other girls, I didn't envy her: I revelled in her popularity, recognising that my lack of social success was nobody's fault but my own; my unremarkable looks just the luck of the genetic draw.

Our paths diverged when I went to Art College and Stella trained as a beauty therapist, but we sporadically kept in touch. We started hanging out again on a regular basis after I returned to Brighton, our home town, where Stella worked in a health and beauty salon, while I pursued a precarious existence as a freelance illustrator of children's books. It didn't take long before our relationship resumed much the same pattern as it had when we were at school.

Stella had a complicated love life. Although she always had a string of admirers, those she chose to favour were invariably the wrong ones – men who were personable and good-looking, but also extremely self-centred and arrogant, and her romantic entanglements invariably came to grief when she belatedly realised this. That's not to say she wasn't pursued by much nicer men. Aidan Miller, for example, who was at school with us, was infatuated with her for years, but he was too quiet and thoughtful for Stella. Only flashy men with overweening self-confidence stood a chance with her. (Unfortunately, Aidan, whom I always fancied, was never interested in me.)

Some of Stella's discarded lovers, astonished and enraged at being dumped, pursued and harassed her long after she had ended the relationship with them. On such occasions, I performed the roles of confidante, counsellor and mopper-up of tears. (This wasn't entirely altruistic on my part: my friend's unfortunate experiences provided me with a convenient justification for not having a satisfying love life of my own, proving I was better off without).

The frequency of our meetings invariably dwindled when Stella began seeing someone else, then the whole saga would repeat itself. But whichever man she was with, she always remained one of the most important people in my life and I feel numb at the thought that she's no longer here.

Who could have murdered her and attacked me? Could it have been the man in my horrifying vision or someone else? The detective asked me if Stella had quarrelled with anyone, such as a spurned lover or a jealous woman friend. There's certainly no shortage of male candidates to choose from – all of those with whom she had liaisons that ended acrimoniously. But what if I'd imagined that scene in the kitchen and it *wasn't* a man? What if it was a woman? Although Stella had many female friends, it was obvious to me that some of them were desperately jealous of her. Angela Fraser, for example, who was at school with us, had issues with Stella. Although she was ostensibly a close friend of hers, I sensed that she disliked her intensely, especially after Stella had supplanted her in the affections of a man she was seeing. But Angela's Angela Robertson now; she's married with a couple of kids and I find it hard to believe that she, or indeed any woman I know, would be capable of stabbing someone out of jealousy, let alone hitting me on the head with a heavy implement. It's more likely to have been a man.

So who could have done it? *Why* was Stella murdered? What happened that night?

My head throbs with the pain of the injury and the struggle to remember.

# Chapter 5

My stay in the neurological unit is a lengthy one as the injury is apparently serious and could have long-term consequences.

The treatment is gruelling. I have X-rays of the inside of my head and CT and MRI scans to check for brain damage. A tube is inserted into my skull to monitor pressure and I'm given a procedure that measures and records the electrical activity in my brain.

As the days go by, I'm visited by a succession of different specialists – a neuropsychologist, a physiotherapist and an occupational therapist.

I'm given a series of tests to check my muscles, reflexes and balance. My memory is of particular concern. Someone regularly comes into my room and asks me a series of simple questions such as: What is your name and address? What year is it? What is the name of the current prime minister?

I have no difficulty answering these questions, but cannot for the life of me recall anything about the incident that caused me to be brought to the hospital in the first place. All I know for sure is what the detective has told me: someone viciously attacked Stella then me, not long after her birthday party had ended. Everything else is a complete blank. This is apparently due to "post traumatic amnesia" and "retrograde amnesia" – lost memory relating to events prior to an injury. Nobody is able to tell me how long such conditions will last. They say it depends on the individual.

Unfortunately my recovery is impeded by the shock of learning about Stella's murder. Overwhelmed with misery and despair, I feel exhausted and fragile. I find it difficult to sleep and when I do briefly doze off, I have a recurrent nightmare in which a man with his back to me is bending over Stella's supine form.

I have no appetite and because my throat is so sore, the nurses have put me on a liquid diet – a bland-tasting protein drink that almost makes me gag.

It's only very slowly that I start to regain my strength, and when I'm judged fit enough, I'm moved to a Neuro Rehabilitation Centre where I'm given a bright but rather bare single room. While I'm here, the detective visits me again and shows me a list of the people who were at Stella's party. I assume the police will have questioned all of them by now, but he doesn't mention this or disclose any information they may have revealed. He tells me their names have been checked against a guest list that was found in Stella's flat, and asks if I think anyone is missing from it.

'Did anybody turn up unexpectedly, or arrive after all the others had left?'

'I'm afraid I still can't remember.' (I wonder if some events are just too *awful* to remember).

DI Forrester asks me to look specifically at the names of the male guests to see if any of them will jog my memory. 'Was one of them the man you saw leaning over Stella?'

I squint at the names but none of them seems to belong to the man in my nightmare vision. 'I don't know. I'm sorry.'

He looks disappointed. 'Perhaps you might recognise him if I bring some photographs to show you?'

'Perhaps.'

He waits for a moment, then asks, 'Have you recalled any details about the party yet, Hanna? Anything at all, no matter how small or insignificant it may seem?'

'No. I'm sorry.' I feel irritated at being repeatedly asked the same question. And why do I feel I have to keep apologising for my loss of memory when it's obviously not my fault?

'You don't remember anyone having words with Stella that evening? Any altercation; any arguments?'

'No. You asked me that before.'

'What about you? Did you have any arguments with her that night or beforehand?'

I'm astonished at the question. 'Me? Why?'

'You got on well with each other?'

'Of course! Stella is...*was*... one of my closest friends. We met at primary school; grew up together.'

He smiles and his creased face looks suddenly younger. 'Even the closest of friends sometimes argue, Hanna.'

I'm startled, suddenly aware of where this might be leading. I was possibly one of the last people to see Stella alive, but surely he can't think *I* was responsible for what happened to her? My voice trembles. 'You're not implying that *I* had anything to do with--?'

'No, of course not,' he says quickly. 'I'm just trying to establish what mood Stella was in that night; whether she seemed angry or upset; whether there was a situation that arose during the course of the evening that might have escalated; a situation that could have involved anyone who was there; maybe just one person, maybe several.'

'I honestly don't know.'

'So you can't remember whether she was upset about anything – or with anyone – *before* the party?' he asks me yet again.

'You already asked me that too and I keep telling you I don't remember her being upset about anything in particular,' I say irritably, 'at least not that she mentioned to me. Presumably you've already asked the people who were at the party the same question? Their memories of it are bound to be a lot better than mine.'

He nods. 'We're trying to put a picture together from as many of the guests as possible.' He folds and pockets the list and tells me he'll take a formal statement when I'm feeling better and my memory returns.

I decide to ask him a question that's been worrying me. 'If I witnessed Stella being stabbed, why didn't whoever did it stab me as well?'

'Good question. We think – but this is only supposition, mind – that you must have entered the kitchen at the very moment the perpetrator was attacking her, so he – or maybe it was a she – may have panicked and hit you on the head with whatever implement was nearest to hand. Whoever it was must have withdrawn the knife afterwards.'

I shudder. 'Do you know what I was hit with?'

He frowns. 'It was possibly a cast iron skillet. There was one in the kitchen sink after you and Stella were found. It was completely clean so the perpetrator must have washed it to remove any traces of blood and hair, as well as fingerprints of course. It's a heavy utensil...not surprising it did so much damage.'

'A skillet!' The thought that I was hit on the head with a frying pan strikes me as both terrifying and absurd. 'Who

21

found us – me and Stella?'

'Luckily for you, one of the guests – a young woman called Claudia – had lost her keys and went back to the flat to look for them. She found you both in the kitchen and raised the alarm. Do you know her?'

'Yes, she's a beautician at the salon where Stella worked. But you don't think she--'

'No, she's been eliminated as a suspect. As you can imagine she was totally traumatised by the experience. Stella was dead by the time she entered the kitchen and you were in a pretty bad way yourself. It was very fortunate for you that she returned to the flat when she did.'

'Poor Claudia.' I imagine finding Stella and myself lying on the kitchen floor must have been utterly terrifying for the young woman.

A nurse enters and says it's time for me to have some more tests, so the detective departs.

\* \* \*

There are always two men sitting at the door just outside my room and I belatedly discover that they're police guards. It's a security measure, DI Forrester informs me, as I have most likely witnessed a murder. He implies that the person who killed Stella and then attacked me, might try to get at me again to stop me identifying him. He says it's just as well I haven't yet been discharged and when I am, I may have to go into Witness Protection and be moved to a safe house.

The situation seems so unreal that at first I'm not as alarmed as the detective obviously thinks I should be. But when he stresses that whoever hit me on the head might have intended to kill me as well as Stella – and may now want to track me down in order to finish the job – a trickle of cold fear runs down my back. The thought that my attacker could still be on the loose terrifies me.

My few visitors are all strictly vetted, presumably for the same security reasons. I suspect none of the guests who were at the party are allowed to come, although DI Forrester doesn't actually tell me this. My sister Penny – my closest relative since my mother succumbed to cancer two years ago – visits me again, but as she has young children and lives in Birmingham, I don't expect her to undertake the journey a third time.

Maria, a woman who lives in the same block as me, comes to see me several times. She has a spare key to my flat and offers to keep an eye on it while I'm marooned here. I accept the offer gratefully and ask her to bring me various items I need: nightclothes, toiletries, my post and, crucially, my mobile phone and charger. I have now begun to worry about my work – a commission to illustrate a book I should have started on. I was too weak to think about it before. I call the publishers and alert them to the enforced delay.

A succession of other friends and acquaintances come to see me but conversation is awkward and spasmodic and they don't stay for long.

I'm surprised one afternoon when Stella's elderly parents enter my room. I've known the couple for years and am fond of them. They were kind to me when I was a child, and I used to spend a lot of time at their home which was more comfortable and warmer – in every sense of the word – than my own. But it's a painful visit. The tragedy of losing their only daughter has aged them visibly. They both seem extremely frail and their expressions are haunted. Her father can barely speak and when her mother grasps my hand, she bursts into tears. 'Who was it, Hanna?' she asks in a quavering voice after she manages to get her emotion under control. 'Do you know who did it? Did you see who it was?'

'I'm sorry, Mrs Knight. I'm afraid I can't remember anything at all about what happened that night.'

'Was it one of those awful men she was involved with? Was it Hugh?'

'I really don't know.' I recall that Stella's parents – in many ways more discerning than she was – were often appalled by their daughter's choice of male partners. They particularly disapproved of her marriage to a man considerably older than herself with two divorces behind him.

I tell the old couple that I'm suffering from a traumatic brain injury that has affected my memory.

'But you will recover your memory, won't you?' Stella's father asks.

'I'm not sure. Nobody seems to know.'

He shakes his head. 'We need to find out who... why...why anyone would...do such a thing.' His voice tails off and he stares helplessly into the distance.

'The police have assigned a family liaison officer to us,' adds his wife. 'He's very kind, but what can he do? He says they're pulling out all the stops to find the person who did it, but that's not going to bring Stella back, is it?'

I wonder whether discovering who killed Stella and why, will actually lessen their grief and pain. I suspect not. They both worshipped their beautiful daughter although, after they moved to the country near Hassocks some years ago, I couldn't fail to notice that she neglected them, visiting them rarely and usually only when she needed their help or a refuge from one of her disastrous relationships.

# Chapter 6

I'm still in the rehabilitation centre when Stella's funeral takes place. It's a while after her death as there had to be a post mortem and inquest, but despite my pleading, the medics insist I'm not fit enough to attend. I'm devastated at not being able to say a proper goodbye to my oldest friend.

DI Forrester comes to see me a few days after the event and shows me video footage of the mourners waiting outside the crematorium before and after the ceremony. He freezes some of the frames and asks which individuals I recognise.

I squint at the images of people talking together in small groups and peering at the floral tributes. Although there are a number of mourners that I don't recognise, I'm able to indicate several of Stella's colleagues and some of her friends. I'm slightly surprised to see JC among them. He never rated Stella. But I suppose when one of your contemporaries dies prematurely and in such horrendous circumstances, you'd feel you had to pay your respects, wouldn't you? I'm also surprised to see Hugh Whitmore, Stella's former husband, standing stony-faced on his own by the crematorium door. Aidan Miller is among the mourners of course, and another familiar figure is Angela – our former schoolmate – with her burly husband Ian Robertson. She's weeping ostentatiously as she examines the wreaths displayed on a wall outside the crematorium. Rather uncharitably, I wonder if the tears were completely genuine.

The detective now shows me photographs of all the men who attended Stella's birthday party. 'Can you take a look at these? Is one of them the man you think you saw standing over Stella in her kitchen?'

I study the faces of the men in the photos. Most of them I recognise but I can't identify any of them as the person in my horrendous vision.

The detective puts the photos away with an air of disappointment. He asks me about Stella's former lovers and the nature of her relationships with them. As I was one of her closest friends, he believes I may be able to give him some useful information. He's particularly interested in what I can recall about two of Stella's longer-term partners, Steve Cottram and Damian Matthews, and about Hugh Whitmore, the man she was married to for over three years.

Although I still can't recall anything about the birthday party and its aftermath, I have no difficulty remembering earlier situations and events, so I'm relieved that I can finally answer at least some of the detective's questions.

\* \* \*

Stella fell in love with Steve Cottram a year or so after my return to Brighton. Charming and flirtatious, he was tall with dark wavy hair, a hooked Roman nose and even white teeth.

Steve was a software designer and consultant whose work often took him to different parts of the country to fulfil short-term contracts. I believe the frequency of his absences was one of the reasons why Stella's relationship with him lasted longer than many of the others. Another was that, like her, Steve had expensive tastes: he loved designer clothes and top-of-the-range cars; patronised exclusive clubs and restaurants, stayed at five-star hotels and always had the most expensive seats at prestigious sports and music events. With such a lifestyle, he needed a ravishing girlfriend on his arm and Stella fitted the bill admirably, although I doubt they had much in common apart from a joint taste for luxury. I had strong misgivings when, not long after the relationship started, she left her rented flat and moved in with him.

Occasionally, when Steve's work commitments brought him back to Brighton, Stella would invite me to join the two of them for drinks or special occasions, and there were a few toe-curling evenings when one of his friends was brought along as a blind date for me, usually someone to whom I took an instant dislike, and doubtless vice versa.

I never took to Steve either. I disliked his arrogance and the way he talked down to Stella, sometimes ridiculing her in company, although she was so under his spell in the early stages of their relationship that she never seemed to notice or mind. It's true she wasn't the sharpest knife in the drawer, but that was no reason to patronise her and deride her occasional shows of ignorance in front of others, especially as Steve was essentially misogynistic and, like most misogynistic men, loathed and feared any women he considered "too" clever or intelligent.

After Steve and Stella had been living together for about eighteen months, I began to notice a change in her. She appeared strained and occasionally had bruises on her face and arms that she attempted to conceal with flesh-coloured make-up from the salon where she worked. I wasn't fooled when she tried to pass these off as the results of silly accidents.

'If he's violent, you should report him to the police and leave him,' I advised her more than once, but she always angrily denied that Steve was abusive towards her and after a while, I began to see increasingly less of her. She no longer made arrangements to meet me for lunch or a drink and was evasive when I rang her. I suspected that Steve was preventing her from seeing me, and not only me: several of her other friends told me that they'd also lost contact with her.

It took over a year before things came to a head. One night Stella unexpectedly called round at my flat. Her eyes were red, her lip was swollen and she looked uncharacteristically dishevelled. She told me tearfully that she'd had an almighty row with Steve who'd accused her of wearing revealing clothes, flirting with other men and coming home suspiciously late after work in the evenings. She said he'd been interrogating her about what she "got up to" during the times when he was working away, demanding to know where she went and who she spent time with. Several times she'd discovered him surreptitiously checking her phone. She asked me if she could stay the night and of course I agreed, but I wasn't surprised when Steve came banging on my door in the early hours. Nor was I surprised when, after an alternately stormy and tearful exchange between the two of them, Stella meekly returned with him to the luxury flat they shared in Kemptown. I suspected that they wouldn't be sharing it for much longer.

Steve held me to blame when Stella, far too belatedly in my opinion, decided she'd had enough. Their rows had become increasingly frequent and when she realised she was enjoying his absences more than his presence, she decided to call it a day and moved out of the flat.

That was when Steve started ringing me at all hours of the day and night. The gist of what he accused me of (using language I wouldn't care to repeat), was that I was a malign influence on her. It was I, he claimed, who had persuaded Stella to leave him; she would never have done that of her own volition. I was an "effing lesbian" and worse.

I blocked his number on my phone but he sometimes came and pounded on my door late at night, shouting drunken abuse. When this had gone on for a while, I went to the police and he was given a caution.

Stella meanwhile had taken refuge with her parents who by then had moved to a cottage in the country. They protected her from Steve, as did her colleagues at the salon, one of whom used to accompany her to her car after work whenever she discovered that Steve was back in Brighton after a period working away. I suspect she never appreciated the extent to which he took his resentment towards her out on me.

* * *

'Was Cottram regularly violent towards her?' DI Forrester asks. Sitting with me in my room in the Rehabilitation Centre, he's been listening attentively and making notes while I dredged up everything I could remember about Stella's relationship with Steve.

'I think he probably was. When she was living with him she often used to have bruises she claimed were accidents. It was only after they split up that she told me just how abusive and controlling he'd been, but I think she was too ashamed or too proud to admit that he hit her on a regular basis.'

'You don't think she was into S and M?'

'Good God, no!'

He taps his teeth thoughtfully with his pen. 'Would you have known whether she was or not?'

'Yes, I would have known.' I can't suppress a smile, for Stella, despite her woeful experience of men, persisted in retaining a totally unrealistic "hearts and flowers" view of male-female relationships. She used to accuse me of being a cynic if I ever commented on her naivety.

'How long did he go on harassing her?'

'For several months. He thought he was God's gift and couldn't accept that a woman would ever dream of leaving him. He was convinced she'd go back to him eventually. But that all happened long ago. Steve faded out of the picture when she started seeing Damian Matthews.'

'Tell me about him.'

\* \* \*

Unfortunately the situation with Steve became a pattern – a template – for most of Stella's subsequent relationships. Like Steve, Damian was tall, good-looking and superficially charming. He had ginger hair, a lopsided, quizzical smile, and what Stella once described to me as "come to bed" hazel eyes. After they became "an item", it didn't take long for alarm bells to start ringing in my head.

Damian was a freelance producer of documentary films and, I subsequently discovered, an inveterate gambler who regularly used to borrow money from Stella which I suspect he never repaid. I was dismayed when, after they'd been seeing each other for about six months, she gave up her new flat and moved in with him.

She seemed happy enough in the relationship at first, but after a year or so passed, she became anxious and subdued. On the infrequent occasions when I met up with the two of them, I noticed that Damian often acted in a curt and dismissive way towards her. He seemed almost as controlling as Steve had been, although I didn't detect any signs of physical violence.

'Damian's nothing like Steve,' Stella insisted when I voiced my concerns. 'He gets depressed, that's all; it's frustrating and stressful for him constantly having to secure new commissions.'

'And the gambling?'

But whenever I mentioned Damian's gambling, she would clam up and refuse to discuss it.

As time went on, however, things didn't seem to improve and on the last few occasions I saw them together, it was obvious that the relationship had turned irreparably sour. Steve was morose and tightlipped and Stella appeared constantly nervous in his company. When I subsequently questioned her, she again made excuses for his bad mood: the commissions weren't coming in as often as they used to; money was tight; he had been drinking heavily…

'He shouldn't take any of that out on you,' I protested.

But Stella didn't listen. Once again, she hung on until she came to the belated conclusion that life with Damian had become intolerable. At that point she moved out of his flat and retreated a second time to the country to stay with her parents. Damian pursued her with abusive texts and phone calls and took to hanging around outside the salon where she worked, harassing her and intimidating clients. She was finally persuaded to go to the police when he started posting intimate pictures of her on social media sites. Like Steve, Damian was given a caution and he backed off. It took Stella some time to recover from the unpleasantness but, as usual, she eventually bounced back.

* * *

'How long ago was this?' D I Forrester asks, rapidly scribbling notes.

I try to think. 'Six, maybe seven years.'

'Did Matthews bother her again?'

'I don't think so. He stopped after she made a formal complaint and the police gave him a caution.'

'Yes, we have the details on file.' He finishes writing and looks up at me. 'Have you seen him since that time?'

'No, I never came across him again. We didn't exactly move in the same circles.'

The detective frowns. 'I gather he accumulated some bad debts; moved in unsavoury company and eventually left the area but…' he flips through his notebook '… didn't leave any forwarding details at his last known address.' He glances up at me. 'Though I gather he's been seen back in Brighton recently.'

'Has he? I've never seen him again and I hope I never do!'

'There were other boyfriends after him?'

'Oh yes, quite a few. Stella always had one after the other. I'm not sure I remember all of them. There was one called Ben, then Chris something or other, but none of them lasted long, until Hugh of course.'

'Hugh Whitmore?'

I sigh 'Yes. Unfortunately.'

# Chapter 7

'For God sake don't move in with this one!' I warned her, but Stella did worse than that. She married him!

Hugh Whitmore was a mixture of both Steve and Damian – handsome, charismatic, smooth-tongued and totally ruthless. A property developer, he'd founded *Whitmore Futures Ltd*, a local company which produced planning schemes that looked deceptively attractive in graphic and digital presentations, but were completely out of harmony with the areas of the city for which they were designed. Even so, following brief and scantily publicised consultations, the plans were almost always approved by the council planning committee after Hugh had offered "sweeteners" intended to benefit the communities destined to receive the new developments. The resulting blocks of extortionately-priced luxury flats usually included a smattering of "affordable" residential units that were anything but affordable. Despite the fact that several *Whitmore Futures* building developments required major structural repairs a mere few years after they were erected, Hugh never failed to have a number of other grandiose planning schemes in the pipeline.

He had already been married twice before he started dating Stella, both unions having ended in long drawn-out and acrimonious divorces, in the course of which his former wives were granted custody of the children resulting from the relationships. Anyone could see that Stella was making a terrible mistake, but she was so besotted with Hugh that she chose to ignore his reputation and to believe his claim that his previous spouses were "bitches from hell".

One evening, a month or so after she and Hugh had announced that they intended to marry, I made a last-ditch effort to make her see sense.

I'd called on her in the flat she was temporarily renting above the salon where she worked, and found her perched on the sofa, flicking through a magazine containing photographs of expensive wedding dresses and accessories.

As soon as I entered the room, Stella thrust a picture of a skin-tight, floor-length white gown in front of my eyes. 'What do you think of this one? I'd like to get something like this.'

I pushed the magazine impatiently aside for there was no way I could disguise my uneasiness about the forthcoming nuptials. 'Look,' I said, 'don't you think this wedding is far too soon? You've hardly known the man five minutes. Are you sure you're doing the right thing?'

Stung by my lack of interest, Stella slapped the magazine down on the coffee table. 'Of course I'm doing the right thing,' she declared huffily. 'Why? Don't you approve of marriage, Hanna?'

I shrugged. 'I don't see the point. Why not just live together? At least it would be easier to extricate yourself when it comes to a sticky end like all your previous relationships.'

She winced. 'That's the trouble with you, Hanna Walker. You don't have a romantic bone in your body!'

'And the trouble with you, Stella Knight, is that you don't have a realistic bone in yours! With your record, what makes you think this relationship is going to last longer than any of the others?'

She gave a theatrical sigh. 'Because Hugh is just …perfect.'

'Huh!' I snorted. 'I bet you thought exactly the same when you were seeing Steve and Damian.'

'No, it wasn't the same with them. Neither of them was…right.' Her face assumed a dreamy expression. 'This time it's for real; it's forever.'

'I'll remind you of that when it all goes wrong,' I muttered uncharitably. 'But don't you think it's ominous that Hugh has already been married twice and both times it ended in tears?'

'I'm fed up with people saying that.' She wrinkled her nose disdainfully. 'He chose the wrong women, that's all.'

'And you believe you're the right one?'

'Of course.' She tossed her silky hair. 'You're not jealous are you, Hanna? I think you are. You're trying to spoil this for me because you've never met anyone you want to marry…' her lip curled '…or who wants to marry *you*!'

I was needled by the comment because it was true. Nobody *had* ever asked me to marry them. I'd had a few short-lived and unsatisfactory affairs but I'd never been in love or experienced a "grand passion". I wasn't even sure if such a thing as a grand passion existed. Most of the famous ones I'd read about in history and fiction – Anthony and Cleopatra, Romeo and Juliet, Samson and Delilah – came to a tragic end, so I liked to think I'd been spared.

'It's true, nobody's asked me to marry them,' I conceded, 'but that's not the point. This isn't about me, it's about *you*.

Of course I'm not jealous and I'm not trying to spoil anything for you, Stella. I don't want you to make another mistake, that's all.'

She smiled radiantly. 'This isn't a mistake. Hugh's the one; I know it.'

'But he's years older than you.'

'Only fifteen,' she muttered sullenly.

I tried a different tack. 'Well what about his professional reputation? What about all the dodgy developments he's created and those awful flats no-one can afford? Are you sure you want to marry someone who's blighted the city with those monstrosities? Remember Regency Towers - that concrete slab he created that developed cracks in the masonry a year or so ago?'

She flushed. 'It wasn't Hugh's fault things went wrong with that; it was because of dishonest contractors. Hugh's a very successful developer.'

'If you mean by "successful" that he's made a lot of money, that's true, ' I retorted, 'but at whose expense? Most of the flats he's built cost so much to buy or rent that half of them are still empty, and that's at a time when so many people are homeless. Haven't you noticed the number of rough sleepers there are in the city these days?'

She shrugged. 'Well you can't hold Hugh responsible for that. If people can't get their act together and sort themselves out, that's their problem.' She picked up the wedding magazine again, a clear signal that the conversation was over, and started flicking through the pages.

'What do you think of this one?' She held up a picture of another elegant gown for my inspection. 'Do you think it would suit me?'

* * *

The wedding was, predictably, an extremely lavish affair. Stella arrived at the picturesque little country church in a decorated horse-drawn carriage, looking spectacular. Photographers from various celebrity gossip magazines mingled with the guests. The reception was at an exclusive golf club and the lengthy honeymoon was spent at a luxury resort in the West Indies.

I didn't see much of Stella after the happy couple returned to Hugh's palatial house in Hove, but we eventually started meeting up again on an irregular basis, usually for a quick drink in the evenings after she'd finished work at the salon where she was now employed on a limited, part-time basis. (Hugh apparently didn't think it reflected well on him to have a working wife).

She seemed contented enough during the first two years of marriage, but then I started detecting signs that my misgivings were yet again proving correct. They were similar to those I'd noticed when she was living with Steve and Damian – a strained expression on her face and a marked lack of her usual vivacity. Once, when I discovered that she hadn't been at work for several weeks, I called to see her at Hugh's luxury home near Hove Park. Stella came to the door looking pale and I was shocked to see that her face was bruised and there was a sling on her left arm. She told me she'd broken the arm and hurt her cheek after tripping and falling heavily on the front doorstep. The explanation didn't ring true but she reacted angrily when I questioned her and pointed out the similarities with her previous relationships. The injuries forced her to resign from her job and although I rang her numerous times, she always made excuses not to see me.

One night, however, when Hugh was working late, she

called me in tears and confided that life with him was becoming impossible. She said he'd accused her of being unwelcoming to his children when they came for weekends, whereas she'd always been pleasant to them despite their open hostility towards her. She told me that he'd become increasingly violent, had occasionally slapped her and once even kicked her in the stomach. Even worse, on one occasion when they were arguing, he'd pushed her out of his car while it was still moving. He punched her in the face when she threatened to report him to the police and she admitted that she was frightened of him. She also suspected that he was seeing another woman.

Despite the catalogue of abuse Stella described, it was several more months before she summoned enough courage to report Hugh. By then, however, most of the worst bruises had faded and she felt her complaints weren't taken seriously by the police. She said that when they interviewed Hugh, he conducted his usual charm offensive and denied everything, claiming that she was unstable and hysterical and had a tendency to exaggerate. She told me the police appeared to believe him, perhaps because he was such a prominent local businessman. However the fact that she'd made a formal complaint against Hugh inevitably made the domestic situation worse, and finally, nearly four years to the day after tying the knot, she decided to sue for divorce.

I refrained from saying "I told you so" as I derived no satisfaction from being right.

The divorce proceedings were predictably stormy and involved a long period of unpleasant legal wrangling. Having been obliged to pay large settlements to his two previous wives, Hugh had no intention of doing so again, and through various nimble sleights of hand involving his business and tax affairs, he attempted to conceal the full extent of his wealth from the courts to ensure that Stella would get as little as possible. 'Women are vultures,' he informed her, 'and I'll be damned if I'm paying out to any more of you bitches. You won't get a penny from me.'

With financial help from her parents, however, Stella managed to engage a skillful lawyer who succeeded in obliging Hugh to pay her a reasonable settlement. He was also ordered to sign over to her a majority share in a holiday property in the south of France they had acquired during the marriage.

It took her a while to pick herself up after the divorce, but eventually she felt able to move on. With the money Hugh had reluctantly agreed to give her, she acquired co-ownership of a beauty salon in town and rented a garden flat in a large Victorian house. With several live-in partnerships and a divorce behind her, she declared, coming up to the age of forty, that from then on she would remain single. No one believed her of course, least of all me!

The birthday party was intended to be a celebration of her new freedom.

# Chapter 8

'Stella seems to have been a habitual victim,' DI Forrester murmurs, more to himself than to me, after I've exhausted my recollections of her marriage to Hugh.

I reflect on this assessment of Stella for a moment but dismiss it. 'No, I think it was that she was naïve; she kept falling for the same kind of man and always seemed surprised when the relationship turned sour. It was OK when she was just going out with someone, spending money and having fun – clubbing or having lavish holidays – but when it came to living together, it never worked. I don't think Stella fitted her lovers' image of how a wife or partner should be. They probably wanted her to slot into a traditional gender role, but domestic life didn't suit Stella at all; she hated stuff like cooking and housework and was always adamant that she didn't want children. What happened with Hugh was totally predictable, but she wouldn't listen when I and other people warned her not to marry him.'

I feel guilty in case I seem to be defiling Stella's memory, although I expect the detective has heard somewhat similar accounts from other people.

He nods slowly as though confirming my unspoken thoughts. 'So it would seem. Was there anyone after

Whitmore? Other men friends?' His pen is poised above his notebook.

'Not that I knew of. That was pretty unusual for Stella, but I think the divorce left her feeling very bruised.'

'So she wasn't seeing anyone in particular in the period before the party?'

'No, at least I don't think so. She never mentioned anyone to me. And if she had been seeing someone, she probably would have invited him to the party.'

He hesitates before adding, 'Unless he was married.'

'What do you mean?'

'Well if she was seeing someone in secret, she might not have wanted anyone to know.'

This idea had never struck me. 'No I'm sure she wasn't seeing anyone in secret. She would have told me if she was.'

'Would she?' He gazes at me gravely. 'Are you sure?'

'Yes.' I wonder uneasily if the detective knows something about Stella that I don't. In my mind I run through the names of the married men in her circle, but can't think of any in whom she had a particular interest or who was likely to attract her.

'Do you know whether she'd been contacted by Whitmore before the party?' the detective now asks.

I'm surprised. 'Hugh? Not to my knowledge. They were still at daggers drawn.'

'Are you sure?'

I pause to think. 'Well, she did mention that they were in contact once, but that was some time ago, towards the beginning of the year. There was an argument about the holiday home in France she'd acquired the main share in as part of the divorce settlement. Hugh wanted to take his children there during the spring half-term holiday but she objected. As his kids used to give her a lot of grief, she didn't see why she should agree to them using it during school holidays. Why do you ask?'

DI Forrester carefully removes a piece of fluff from his sleeve before answering.

'Because there were a number of messages from Whitmore on Stella's phone.'

I'm staggered. 'Messages from *Hugh*?'

'They were made during the weeks leading up to the party. You didn't know about them?'

'I had no idea. Stella never said anything to me about Hugh contacting her. But she was aware of what I thought of him, so she may not have wanted me to know. What were the messages about?'

He glances down at his notes then back at me. 'They were brief but relatively amicable, implying that the two of them were on... somewhat *friendlier* terms than an argument about a holiday home suggests.'

'*Amicable*?' I can't believe what I'm hearing. 'That's impossible! Stella *hated* Hugh because of the way he acted during the marriage and how difficult he was about the divorce settlement.'

The detective's thick eyebrows rise, lending his face an almost comical expression of surprise. 'In that case it appears your friend may have been keeping rather a lot from you.'

I'm too shocked to answer.

He gazes at me thoughtfully for a second then produces a photo from a folder. 'Do you recognise this car?'

He shows me a photo of a very smart-looking silver car, caught in the light of a streetlamp.

'No. Should I? It looks very expensive.'

'It *is* very expensive; it's a *Lexus RX*. It was caught on

CCTV on the night of the party, not once, but twice, not that far from where Stella lived. It was parked round a corner, near the top of her road. Do you know who it belongs to?'

'No. Who?'

He gives a grim sort of smile. 'It belongs to Stella's ex husband, Hugh Whitmore.'

'It's *Hugh's* car?' The information takes a moment to sink in, although I shouldn't be surprised as the model is exactly the type of car Hugh used to drive. 'Are you sure it's his?'

'Absolutely.'

'You mean…Did he…Did he go to Stella's flat that night?'

'Unfortunately the door of the building is out of the camera's range.'

'But does it mean that Hugh could be the one who …you know…?'

He shakes his head. 'It's not possible to draw that conclusion. The tapes from that night are still being examined. But we also have CCTV footage from the other end of the street where Stella lived. The camera there caught a different man – not Whitmore – walking in the direction of the flat a short time after the party had ended. Again, we don't know whether he actually went into the building or not.' He rummages in the folder and extracts another photo. 'Do you recognise this person?'

He shows me a photo of a dark figure, caught mid stride.

I squint at it. Although the man looks slightly familiar, I don't recognise him. 'No, sorry; I don't know who that is.'

The detective departs shortly afterwards, leaving me to reflect on the disturbing information he's just divulged. Why didn't Stella tell me that Hugh had contacted her before the party? I find it impossible to believe that they were on friendly terms after the bitter hostilities of the divorce which was only just over a year ago. If his car was parked near the top of the road she lived in on the night of the party, could he have gone to the flat after the guests had left? If so, why? Could Hugh Whitmore be the man in my nightmare vision? Was he the man I either imagined or remembered, leaning over Stella when she was lying on the floor with blood on her dress? It's not impossible as it's on record that he was violent towards her during the marriage.

The thought that Hugh may have been the person who killed Stella and attacked me, makes me shiver. I assume the police must have already questioned him. The fact that he, like several others of her "significant" exes, was reported for domestic abuse and harassment would surely automatically result in his being considered a "person of interest".

In the evening I watch a televised broadcast of a press conference in which the senior investigating officer leading the murder enquiry admits that they don't yet have a clear idea of who killed Stella. In response to questions, he insists that the investigation is being extremely thorough and claims his team is following various "promising lines of enquiry".

What are they? I wonder.

# Chapter 9

When DI Forrester next visits me at the Rehab Centre, he looks unusually pleased. 'Whitmore has admitted going to Stella's flat on the night of the party,' he declares. 'He owned up after we told him we have tapes showing his *Lexus* in a parking bay near the top end of her road.'

I gasp. 'You mean it *was* Hugh who killed Stella and then attacked me?'

'There's no evidence of that, but we now have a clearer idea of his movements that night.' He gets out a notebook and finds a page. 'I wonder if any of this will ring a bell, Hanna. The tapes show him parking the car at about 9.30pm, getting out and walking in the direction of the building where Stella lived – the camera's range doesn't extend as far as the door – then returning about ten minutes later and driving away. Just before midnight, he returns and parks in the same place; he sits in the car for a while, then gets out and again walks down the road towards her building. He returns to the car some thirty or so minutes later.'

The detective falls silent as he waits for my reaction.

My heart thuds as I ponder the implication of what he's just told me.

'You don't remember Whitmore turning up at Stella's

flat?'

I shake my head. 'No, I still have no recollection whatsoever of that night. But why did he go there twice?'

'He claims he wanted to give Stella a birthday present.'

'A *birthday present*?' I'm incredulous. 'He didn't want to give her a penny after they got divorced. She would have been destitute if he'd had his way. I can't believe he'd buy her anything.'

'Nevertheless he said he'd got her a gift and admitted he'd been in contact with her for some weeks before the party; he claimed he'd realised she was "the love of his life" and was hoping to persuade her to go back to him!' The detective ignores my sceptical snort. 'He believed she was coming round to the idea.'

'That's absolutely ridiculous!'

'Not according to Whitmore: absence makes the heart grow fonder and all that.'

DI Forrester gives me a searching look. 'None of this prompts any memories? You weren't aware they were considering getting back together?'

I utter a yelp of outrage. 'Absolutely not. Not after the abuse she suffered during the marriage and the way he behaved during the divorce proceedings. The idea almost makes me feel ill.'

'And she never mentioned anything about their recent communication to you?'

'I've already told you; Stella never said that Hugh had been in touch with her. And I don't believe for a second that she would *ever* have considered getting back with him. Not after his behaviour.'

The detective smiles rather quizzically but says nothing.

'If it's true that he only wanted to give her a present,' I

continue, 'why did he need to go to the flat twice?'

'He says the first time he went, he discovered there was a party going on – it took place the night before her actual birthday I believe – so he waited until he thought the celebration was over. When all the guests had left, he returned to the flat. The front door was still unlocked apparently. And maybe this bit will jog your memory. Whitmore said when he entered the flat he found Stella in the hall and followed her into the kitchen. He said they kissed and …' the detective gives a sardonic laugh '… "fooled around a bit" was the way he put it.'

'Christ! This gets worse. Did he mention that I was still in the flat?'

'Yes. He said you were tidying up after the party and kept coming into the kitchen with trays of dirty plates and glasses. He told us you weren't at all pleased to see him.'

'I bet I wasn't!'

'He claims your reaction to seeing him there was one of the reasons he didn't stay for long, another being that Stella had apparently had far too much to drink. So he decided to leave, but only after she agreed to meet him the following morning.'

It's my turn to laugh. 'And you believe that?'

'Well, it certainly looks bad, but at the moment we don't have any concrete evidence that it was Whitmore who attacked her; not enough to charge him, at least not enough that will stand up in court. Unfortunately we have no potential witnesses apart from yourself and we can only question him for so long.' He glances hopefully at me. 'I don't suppose --?'

'I'm sorry. I still can't remember anything about that night.' Once again I'm overwhelmed with guilt at not being able to supply the crucial evidence the police need.

'Pity.' He's silent for a moment, then adds, 'There's a carving knife missing from the set in Stella's kitchen, so we're guessing that could have been the weapon. Do you recall the knife?'

I try to visualise Stella's kitchen. 'I know she had a set of carving knives. It was attached to a bracket on the kitchen wall.'

I remember Stella laughing when she showed the knives to me. They were an unwanted Christmas gift and she said as she didn't cook, she would never use them (and to my knowledge, never did). What an irony if she was murdered with one of them.

'Have you found the knife?' I ask the detective.

He sighs. 'Unfortunately not. And something else is missing as well.'

'What?'

'Whitmore said the birthday present he gave Stella was an expensive diamond pendant.'

I give a derisive snort.

'You don't remember seeing it?'

'No. I keep telling you I don't remember anything about that night.'

'He said it was in the shape of a rose.'

'Well he certainly knew that Stella loved roses. There were a number of rose bushes in their garden in Hove.' I remember seeing a lovely photo of her standing next to one of them when it was in early bloom.

'The pendant wasn't on Stella's person when she was found,' the detective tells me. 'It wasn't in the kitchen or anywhere else in the flat.'

I shrug. 'He probably took it back after he killed her.'

'We don't know that Whitmore *did* kill her, Hanna. He claims Stella was delighted with the pendant and he *didn't* take it back.'

'Well he could have been lying. Maybe there was no pendant.'

'In that case, why bother to mention it? He gave us the name of the shop where he bought the item, knowing we'd go there to verify that he actually made the purchase.'

DI Forrester is still regarding me closely and I have a sudden pang of anxiety. Surely he can't think that *I* took the pendant!

'It does seem odd that it's missing.' I stammer.

'Indeed.'

'Claudia didn't see it when she went back for her keys?'

'She says she didn't, and we're inclined to believe her. She must have been in shock when she found you both; certainly not in a fit state to notice anything like a pendant on Stella's person.' He starts to get up for his chair but changes his mind and sits down again. 'Hanna, I know I've asked you this before, but just in case anything has come back to you: did you notice whether Stella seemed nervous or anxious before the party?'

'Not particularly, though she was a bit strung-up – hyper– for a week or so beforehand. I assumed that was from the stress of having to organise it.'

His thick black eyebrows knit together in a frown. 'It's such a pity you still can't remember anything about that night, Hanna. It could make all the difference to the case.'

He looks so mournful that I feel almost sorry for him. 'I know. I really wish I could be of more help.'

He sighs. 'We can only charge Whitmore if we have enough evidence for a realistic prospect of conviction.

Otherwise the court will throw it out. If we don't get any answers in the next day or two we'll have to release him under investigation.'

He again rises to his feet and before leaving, reminds me for the umpteenth time to contact him the moment I recall anything about the party.

After the detective has gone, I find myself trembling with shock. It seems reasonably clear to me now that it must have been Hugh Whitmore, Stella's ex husband, who killed her and then struck me on the head. I always thought Hugh was a bastard but I would never have considered him capable of murder. I still find it curious that Stella didn't tell me she'd been in contact with him. Maybe she thought I'd disapprove, and if that was the case, she would have been right!

One of the details DI Forrester disclosed strikes me as intriguing. If Hugh was telling the truth about giving Stella an expensive pendant, who could have taken it? Like the detective, I don't think it could have been Claudia, the young beautician who stumbled upon the prostrate forms of Stella and myself in the kitchen. On the other hand, the story of the missing jewel could be a fiction; a ploy Hugh dreamed up in the hope that it might suggest that whoever took it off Stella was the person who attacked us both. But this scenario seems far-fetched and I'm now convinced that the police are questioning the right man.

# Chapter 10

Although my injury is healing well on the outside, my brain is still affected and my memory still impaired. I'm told that people suffering from retrograde amnesia – lost memory relating to events prior to an injury – can continue to have problems for a long period, perhaps even forever. The prospect worries and depresses me. It's devastating to think that what was intended as a happy event has had such drastic consequences for me as well as Stella.

Whereas I have no memory of the birthday party itself, incidents and occasions that happened before the event have been returning to me. I have a clear memory, for example, of being with Stella when she was compiling her guest list.

By then she had moved into a large garden flat in the centre of town and when I called on her, I found her going through names and calculating the number of people her living room could comfortably accommodate. Reclining elegantly on the sofa, a glass of wine in her left hand and a pen in her right, she was writing the list on a pad balanced on her knees. I remember gazing at her admiringly. Her beauty, now that she was coming up to forty, was still breathtaking. She still had those huge, almost navy, eyes, wheat-coloured hair and the fabulous slender figure I'd always envied.

She poured me a glass of wine then read out the last names she'd jotted down. I noticed they included several of her old admirers, men she'd dated before Hugh (but not, unsurprisingly, Steve Cottram or Damian Matthews).

'I suppose I ought to ask the Robertsons,' she commented. 'Ian's OK, but I can't stand Angela.'

I was surprised as I remembered Ian was a crony of Hugh's. 'I thought Angela was your friend.'

'Was! Too full of herself by half now she's produced a couple of kids.'

'What's wrong with having a couple of kids?'

She wrinkled her nose. 'Nothing, as long as you don't talk about them all the time as if they're the eighth and ninth wonders of the world!' She checked the list again and chewed the end of her pen. 'I haven't got enough men, unattached ones that is. Do you think I should ask Aidan Miller? I haven't seen him for ages.'

I experienced a stab of pleasure at the thought of seeing Aidan again. 'It's up to you. He may not want to come after you turned him down so often.'

She shrugged. 'That was years ago. Anyway, he married someone else in the end, didn't he?'

'Yes, but they were divorced last year. Didn't his wife go off with another man?'

'That's what I heard. I wasn't surprised. Aidan's rather dull, much too serious if you ask me, but I need some unattached men so I may as well put him on the list.' She scribbled on her pad. 'And what about JC? Should I ask him?'

I was surprised as JC had never been a particular friend of hers. I occasionally bumped into him in town. He was married to a nurse and had two children. 'If you do, you'll have to invite his wife, Sarah, as well,' I advised her.

She peered at the list and stabbed the names with a finger as she counted them again. 'In that case maybe not! I've got enough women already. If I ask Aidan, that already makes forty, exactly the right number for celebrating my fortieth, don't you think? I'm not sure there's room to cram anybody else in anyway. Take a look.' She handed me the list.

Glancing at the names on it – many belonging to friends of Stella's that I didn't particularly like – I uttered an inward groan. I wasn't looking forward to the party at all but Stella insisted she would need my help with passing food around and making sure everyone had drinks.

I sighed. 'Are you sure you need me? You know I'm no good at parties.'

'It'll do you good to come; you're becoming a recluse.' She wagged a finger at me. 'And don't go rushing off early like you usually do. I'll need help with the clearing up after it's over.' She grinned, noticing the expression on my face. 'Don't worry, it won't end late. We can't do anything after midnight in this building. That miserable cow upstairs would complain again.'

# Chapter 11

'There's something I want to ask you, Hanna.' The detective is waiting at the door of my room when I return from a series of medical tests. His expression is serious.

'Oh?' I'm feeling reasonably cheerful today as I've been told I'll soon be fit enough to be discharged. 'What is it?'

'A favour, but I'm afraid it's a big ask.' He eyes me rather uncertainly. 'I know this will be difficult for you, but it could really help the investigation. Would you agree to come with us on a short visit to Stella's flat? It could jog your memory. The medics say you're fit enough to go out on a short accompanied outing, but only if you feel up to it, of course.'

'Oh no, I couldn't!' The prospect of revisiting Stella's flat and seeing the kitchen where she was murdered and I was seriously assaulted, horrifies me.

'I realise it's a lot to ask, but you're a key witness in the case – indeed *the* key witness– and, as I say, it might jog your memory. It need only be a quick visit.' He smiles at me winningly. 'I'd be with you the whole time, and so would DS Hargreaves. We'd make sure you were OK. What do you say, Hanna? Do you think you could do it? We'd be really grateful.'

'No. I'm sorry, but I really don't want to go back there.

You must realise why.' My cheerful mood has completely evaporated.

He looks disappointed. 'I appreciate how difficult it would be after what happened to you, but going back to the flat could help your memory to return as well as assist the murder enquiry. I don't want you to feel pushed into anything but please have a think about it.'

I take a deep breath. I can't think of anything worse than visiting the scene of Stella's brutal murder but feel under pressure. 'Well, if you really think it might help… though I can't guarantee that I'll remember anything …'

He looks pleased. 'Thank you, Hanna. That's very brave. Don't worry. I promise we'll look after you.'

I take a deep breath. 'When do you want me to go?'

'Tomorrow?'

'So soon?' I'm seized with panic.

\* \* \*

The drive to Stella's flat only takes about twenty minutes but it totally exhausts me. It's the first time I've been out of the hospital in weeks and being transported through the streets in the back of a police car, I feel disoriented – weird – almost as if I'm another person watching myself from a distance. When we arrive at the house where Stella used to live, it's with extreme reluctance that, assisted by the detective, I haul myself out of the car.

DI Forrester and a woman officer accompany me as I slowly enter the flat that Stella rented after her divorce from Hugh. It's no longer a crime scene as the forensic team finished their work some time ago, and I'm surprised to see that it looks as if it's been left exactly as it was on the night of the party.

'Nothing's been disturbed,' the detective informs me, 'although the kitchen floor has been cleaned of course.'

My heart beats painfully as we enter the living room. A sob catches in my throat when I spot the birthday cards still displayed on a shelf, the single balloon, emblazoned with the figure 40, dangling forlornly from the ceiling, and the pile of partially-opened gifts on the table. The brightly coloured wrapping paper seems like a mockery: a celebration of a birthday that turned out to be a deathday.

*Stella, the party was supposed to be the start of a new phase of life for you.*

I gaze at the sofa where, not that long ago, Stella was gaily compiling her party guest list; at the fluffy cushions she chose at *Liberty's* after she moved into the flat; at the paintings of Tuscany, one of her favourite places, on the walls (she'd been planning a villa holiday there next spring, and had invited me to go along). I stare at the framed photographs on top of the bookcase: Stella at Ascot; Stella at a wedding; Stella at a local garden party. In all of them her lovely face is wreathed in happy smiles.

Followed discreetly by the two police officers, I force myself to enter the kitchen and stand just inside the door, almost paralysed with horror. Yet as I look around, everything appears completely normal. There's nothing to suggest that only a short time ago, Stella was lying bleeding to death on the floor while I lay badly injured, not that far away from her.

Cleansed of all traces of blood, the kitchen still bears signs of the birthday celebration. The worktops are covered with drinking glasses, stacks of plates and piles of cutlery. They're all sparkling clean as if they've just been washed.

Was that *my* work or did the police do it? Did someone empty the dishwasher?

With a shudder I notice the empty space in the middle of the set of knives mounted on the wall. The skillet the police believe caused my injury is not in evidence. I wonder what else has been removed. I imagine the forensic team must have examined everything in the kitchen extremely thoroughly.

On the kitchen floor there's a crate containing empty champagne bottles, several boxes of empty wine bottles and a black bin bag that appears to be full of discarded beer cans. I wonder whose task it will be to remove all this stuff. And what about Stella's furniture and her personal effects? When the flat is re-let or sold, someone will have to empty the entire contents. Will Stella's parents be up to it? I doubt it, but she doesn't have any other relatives as far as I know.

There's a movement behind me and I become aware of the two police officers hovering in the doorway, obviously hoping that my memory will suddenly and miraculously return.

I close my eyes and try to tune into that fateful night, but nothing comes except a sob, then a paroxysm of weeping.

# Chapter 12

The day finally arrives when I'm discharged from the Rehab Centre. Although I want to go home and am anxious to resume my work – I haven't yet started on a book I've been commissioned to illustrate – I can't help feeling apprehensive about leaving the secure and protective environment of the hospital. I suspect it will be difficult for me to resume normal life after what has happened.

DI Forrester believes that it's safe for me to return to my flat. He tells me Hugh Whitmore has again been remanded in custody and has now been charged with murder although the police are still seeking more evidence.

'You mean you're not sure? What if it turns out that it wasn't him?'

'We're pretty certain we've got the right man,' he reassures me. 'As you know, Whitmore already has a history of domestic abuse, and not just towards Stella; one of his former wives has come forward with information. But don't worry; you're still a key witness and we'll keep an eye on you. Let me know at once if anyone you're not sure of starts hanging around or tries to get in touch with you, or if you receive any suspicious messages. Just a precaution.'

When I leave the hospital, I'm given an information booklet about head injuries. One page has an alarmingly long list of the kind of short- and long-term symptoms I could still experience, and I'm advised to contact my GP immediately if I suffer from any of them. Another page contains a list of support groups set up for victims of head injuries.

A taxi runs me back to my flat. When I get there, I find that Maria, my kind neighbour, has cleaned it in readiness for my return. She has also thoughtfully stocked my kitchen with essential food items and put a vase of flowers on the dining table. Despite these touches, my home feels cold and unwelcoming after being unoccupied for so long, and when I enter the living room, I sink onto the sofa feeling terribly vulnerable and alone. Tears of self-pity flow unchecked down my cheeks. I'm cross with myself as I've never been a weeper. But since waking up in a hospital bed and being told about the vicious assaults on Stella and myself, I've had a number of emotional meltdowns.

* * *

As I expected, I find it difficult to settle back into my former life and feel disoriented. Overwhelmed with gloom and depression, I mooch listlessly around the flat, unable to stop myself dwelling on what has happened. Almost every night I have the same nightmare in which I see a man standing over Stella's lifeless body. Each time I wake up screaming.

As well as anxiety, sleeplessness and sensitivity to noise – all problems I've been warned about – I have become rather absent-minded. Sometimes I can't remember where I've put things or why I've entered a particular room. The booklet I was given at the hospital suggests this is a common reaction after a severe head injury and it may just be temporary, but

I fear my memory could be permanently impaired.

I don't make an appointment to see my doctor as the booklet advises because it would mean taking a bus and at the moment that is too daunting a prospect for me to consider. After spending so long alone in a hospital room, I find going into the streets intimidating. No longer used to traffic and large groups of people, I'm consumed with panic whenever I venture beyond my building. The press of so many people combined with the rush and noise of traffic, creates an excruciating overload on my senses.

My sister calls me every other day to see how I am. I pretend I'm OK as I don't want to worry her. Maria, who comes to check on me most evenings, says how I feel isn't surprising after what I've been through. She sometimes stays to have a glass of wine with me and tries to cheer me up with humorous stories about the diverse people she comes into contact with through her work. A widow several decades older than me, she teaches English to foreign students at a language school in town.

I'm touched by Maria's efforts to lighten my mood, but eventually discover that the solution to my depression is work. After a week has passed, I force myself to make a start on the long-delayed commission to illustrate a children's book. And once I've picked up my art materials again, I find I'm able to distance myself, at least temporarily, from the anxiety and melancholy thoughts that have beset me since I arrived home.

The book is about a young girl who runs away from an unhappy home and is cared for by a tribe of elves. After I draw the girl's face for the first time, I realise with a frisson of unease that she looks uncannily like Stella - the young Stella I knew when we were at school together. I wasn't aware of doing this deliberately, but feel superstitious about changing the face, so leave it as it is.

It's almost two weeks before I feel secure enough to leave the flat on my own without anxiety and panic attacks. But when I do finally venture into town, I find the city looks different. Although it's as busy and vibrant as ever, it seems less attractive – rougher and more run-down than I remember. The streets are litter-strewn and, unless it's my imagination, there are more empty and boarded-up properties than there were before I was admitted to hospital. The main commercial areas are dominated by charity and betting shops, nail bars, fast food joints and coffee bars. Many of the banks, supermarkets and restaurants have grubby sleeping bags, blankets and bundles piled untidily in front of them, and there are more people begging than I recall seeing in the past. It's almost as if I'm viewing the city with new eyes although Maria tells me it's been like this for ages. Perhaps I just didn't notice these things so sharply before.

* * *

I finally summon the courage to visit the Garden of Remembrance where Stella's parents have placed her ashes. It's something I've been feeling apprehensive about but know I need to do.

Maria kindly offers to accompany me to the cemetery. We go there on a sunny Sunday morning and wander around for some time before I spot the plaque I'm looking for. It's brown and inscribed with white writing:

In loving memory of
our dearest daughter
Stella Rose Knight
1978-2018

A bush has been planted next to the plaque, and there's a beautiful bouquet of red roses lying nearby. It has obviously been placed there very recently as the flowers are still fresh. I bend and look at the small card attached to it. The printed message declares that Stella will be forever loved. I assume it's from her parents.

A gardener wanders over and tactfully informs me that no flowers should be left in this area. 'They can be left around the Columbarium, that little flint building over there.' He gestures behind me. I assure him that I will move them.

Maria wanders discreetly away while I weep and bid a final farewell to my beautiful friend.

# Chapter 13

Since I returned to my flat, DI Forrester and a female police officer have been calling round regularly to check on me. I appreciate the added sense of security this provides although I feel I still need to apologise for not remembering anything about the night of the party.

On one of their visits, the detective enquires whether I've received any suspicious messages or had any unwelcome visitors since I was discharged from hospital. Fortunately I haven't, although Maria has alerted me to some disturbing anonymous posts on social media sites containing unpleasant innuendoes about Stella and the murder. DI Forrester tells me this isn't uncommon after a serious crime has been committed and asks to see the posts as they may have a bearing on the murder enquiry. 'Never respond to anything like that,' he advises me. 'You can report them to the social media sites concerned as they have procedures for dealing with such things. And if you receive any abusive messages, pass them on to us as the senders could be committing an offence under the heading of "harassment and malicious communications".'

Alarmed, I decide to stop using social media for the time being, although I'll still need to follow up any potential commissions that come via my website.

\* \* \*

One morning I go to a hairdresser and with a certain amount of trepidation, have my hair cut very short to blend in with the new growth where my head was shaved at the hospital. I also buy some new clothes as I've lost a considerable amount of weight. When I try things on, I discover to my joy that I've dropped almost three dress sizes. For the first time in my life, I actually look quite svelte! I wonder how Stella would react if she could see me now. She sometimes used to call me "Tubs". This was hurtful but I tried not to mind too much.

A day or two after the shopping trip, I'm coming out of the main door of the building where I live when I hear a familiar voice hailing me. Turning, I experience a leap of pleasure on seeing Aidan Miller hurrying towards me. Aidan, a surveyor, is of medium height, not much taller than me, and muscular build. He has sharp hazel eyes and floppy fair hair that tends to fall across his forehead. I've always found him rather attractive and although I never begrudged Stella her legion of admirers, I did envy her for Aidan's constant devotion which lasted for years despite the conspicuous lack of reciprocation.

'It *is* you, Hanna,' he says when he arrives at the door. 'I wasn't sure. You look… different.'

'I've had my hair cut,' I mumble unnecessarily, noticing that his own hair has started to thin a little on top.

'Yes, so I see. It suits you.' He regards me critically. 'And --'.

'I've lost a lot of weight,' I say before he can make any embarrassing comments on my reduced girth. 'I… haven't been very well.' I'm not sure whether to expand on this statement as I don't know if he's aware of what happened to me.

He looks concerned. 'I'm sorry. I heard you were in hospital. Have you recovered? How are you now?'

'Much better, thanks.' I run a hand over my newly shorn head, something I've been doing frequently since my visit to the hairdressers as my hair feels springy and pleasant to touch.

His face clouds over. 'What happened to Stella…it's absolutely--'

'Yes it is.' I'm reluctant to talk about the murder as it makes me too emotional. 'How are you doing, Aidan?'

He ignores the question and asks abruptly, 'Did you know Hugh Whitmore's been arrested?'

'Yes.' I'm surprised as I didn't think Hugh's name had been revealed. He's only been referred to as a 55-year-old man on the news. 'How do you know?'

'Everybody knows. It's all over town. Do you think he did it; killed Stella?'

'Yes,' I say decisively, 'I do.'

He stares at me. 'You *know* it was him?'

'I don't know for sure, but it seems likely. He was violent to Stella, you know, when she was married to him.'

'Yes, I heard the rumours,' he mutters. 'Beats me why she married the bastard. Did you actually see him attack Stella that night?'

'No, that is, I don't know whether I saw him or not. I don't remember. I have post traumatic amnesia, you see, from a head injury.'

Aidan looks shocked. 'I'm sorry. Do you know how it happened?'

I decide to put him in the picture. 'Hugh, if it *was* Hugh, must have hit me on the head with something.' I give a weak laugh. 'The police think it was a skillet, would you believe? A frying pan!'

'Jesus!' he exclaims. 'Whitmore attacked you as well?'

'It appears so. Apparently I stayed late after the party was over and may have witnessed what he did to Stella. The police believe that's why I was attacked.'

'But you don't remember him hitting you?'

I sigh at having to explain my amnesia again. People seem to find it strange that I have no memory of what happened at the party. I have the impression that some don't even believe me. 'I don't remember anything at all about that night,' I tell him. 'I can remember things that happened *before* the party, but not the event itself. You were there, weren't you, Aidan? Stella said she was going to invite you.'

'Yes. I was there.'

'A police detective keeps asking me whether Stella quarrelled with anyone that night. But I have no idea whether she did or not. Did you notice anything like that?'

He shakes his head. 'No I didn't. Those of us who were at the party have been interrogated by the police a number of times, and they asked us the same question. I personally didn't hear or see her arguing with anyone, and none of the other guests I've spoken to did either, as far as I know. As I recall, the party went swimmingly.'

'Did it?'

He gazes at me in surprise. 'You don't remember anything about it at all?'

I shake my head. 'No. The whole evening's a complete blank. Apparently that can happen after a trauma caused by an accident or injury. The doctors say I might gradually regain my memory, but it's equally likely I might never remember what happened. Perhaps it's just as well. What happened to Stella is too horrendous to think about. If I did witness someone murdering her, I honestly don't *want* to remember it.'

Aidan nods sympathetically. 'That's understandable. Have you been in touch with anyone else who was at the party, like the Robertsons?'

'The Robertsons? No, why?'

He looks embarrassed. 'I was surprised to see them there, that's all. I thought he was a crony of Whitmore's. I wondered why Stella invited them.'

'Because Angela was her friend, I suppose.' I don't mention that Stella said she preferred Ian to Angela. 'They both went to the funeral.'

'Yes, I saw them there.' His tone is angry. I wonder why.

A large lorry rumbles past and after the noise dies down, we stand facing each other in silence. I feel awkward and can't think of anything else to say. I don't feel I can ask him about his recent divorce in case it's too intrusive, so start to move away.

'I must get on. It was nice seeing you again, Aidan.'

'Hanna,' he says before I've taken a couple of steps. 'Would you care to have a drink with me one evening?'

Astonished, I come to a halt. 'Well, yes, that would be nice.'

We exchange phone numbers and he asks, 'Are you free on Friday?'

'Yes.' I can't pretend I have many social engagements.

'Cool. Shall I meet you at *The Basketmakers*, around 6.30?'

'Fine, I'll see you there.'

I walk away in a cloud of happiness. After all these years,

Aidan Miller has asked me out! But I can't help wondering why he wants to spend time with me. I know I'll be a poor substitute for Stella whom he worshipped and who seemed to represent a kind of feminine ideal for him. Maybe he thinks my long connection with her will help to keep her memory alive.

Over the next few weeks, I bump into a number of other Brighton acquaintances, some of whom were also guests at Stella's party. Their assessment of the event is the same as Aidan's – it went brilliantly; no-one had any arguments, and far from showing any sign of stress, Stella was the life and soul, dancing her heart out until midnight. Several of her friends invite me to meet them for drinks or meals, but not, I believe, for the pleasure of my company. All are eager to find out what I know about the murder, but I'm afraid I'll just have to disappoint them.

I reflect on the irony that my "popularity" still hinges on my connection to Stella, just as it did when she was alive.

# Chapter 14

'Stella was too good-looking for her own good,' JC observes as we sit drinking coffee in a café in the North Laines.

We'd bumped into each other by chance when I came out to take a short morning break – a habit I've recently got into as my work involves such intense concentration.

JC is a short, rather stocky man with a round cherubic face that always seems to be split in a wide smile. It's been good to catch up with him although the encounter has inevitably prompted painful memories of our shared schooldays with Stella. I've already short-circuited his inevitable questions about the party and Hugh's arrest.

'Can anyone be *too* good-looking?' I enquire, thinking this would be an affliction I'd be more than happy to suffer from.

'What I mean is, women who look like Stella tend to attract the wrong kind of men.'

'That's true,' I say, thinking of Stella's succession of arrogant and controlling partners.

JC scrutinises my face. 'You're looking pretty good yourself these days, Hanna, considering what you've been through. Your hair suits you like that.'

'Thanks, JC, but I know there's no comparison!'

As I sip my coffee, I glance around at the other customers

in the café. Some are chatting companionably in small groups while others, sitting on their own, are peering at their phones or tapping busily on tablets and laptops. I find the ambient hum of voices and occasional hiss of the coffee machine comforting. It feels like normal life has resumed at last.

I turn back to JC. 'It was good of you to go to Stella's funeral. I know you weren't her greatest fan.'

He looks slightly embarrassed. 'Well, we were in the same class at school for a few years and as she's the first...that is, the first of us from our year ...to ...erm... it seemed appropriate.'

'I wanted to go to the funeral too but the medics wouldn't let me. They said I wasn't fit enough.' Tears start trickling down my cheeks. Annoyed with myself, I put down my coffee cup and dab at my eyes. I often feel tearful these days and assume it's another effect of the head injury. I used to be strong and stoical (or so I like to think) but the blow to the head seems to have completely altered my personality. I wonder whether I'll ever achieve the relative emotional equilibrium I enjoyed before the fateful event that happened after Stella's birthday party.

JC leans across the table, his expression worried. He puts a hand on my arm. 'I'm sorry, Hanna. Did I say something to upset you? Are you OK?'

'No, you didn't, and yes, I'm OK.' I rummage in my pocket for a tissue, mop my face and blow my nose. 'Sorry, JC; didn't mean to blub, but it's so hard, you know, coming to terms with ... I still can't accept that Stella's not here anymore. It doesn't seem real.'

'Yeah.' He coughs in an embarrassed sort of way, looks away from me, then mutters, 'Look, Hanna, I know you were close to Stella, but I'm afraid she wasn't …she wasn't always that nice … about you.'

'What?' It's as if an icy hand has gripped my heart.

'She could be quite vicious about people. She used to laugh about you behind your back when we were younger. I once heard her call you her "fat friend, Hanna No Mates". I didn't like to mention it before.'

The wretched tears start welling up again. 'So why are you mentioning it now?'

'Because you're probably mourning her as if she was some kind of saint, but she definitely wasn't a saint.' JC's round face has turned slightly pink and he looks crestfallen. 'Sorry, I thought telling you might help.'

'Well it *doesn't*.' I force a careless laugh. 'You know what kids are like; they can be cruel. We probably all said spiteful things about each other when we were younger.'

'Maybe. I'm sorry, Hanna. I shouldn't have said anything.'

'No, you shouldn't. There was no point. It was thoughtless.' Although I've always known JC wasn't the soul of tact, I feel a surge of hot anger towards him.

There's an uncomfortable silence during which, in an attempt to hide the tears that again threaten to cascade down my cheeks, I turn to watch the people passing the café window. They look enviously carefree.

JC's mobile rings and while he's answering it, I dry my eyes and finish drinking my coffee. His revelation about Stella prompts me to think back to the time when she and I were teenagers and best friends, at least so I believed. I knew she could be bitchy about her other friends so I should have realised that I wouldn't be immune from her scathing tongue. In those days she was teasingly affectionate towards me although she was sometimes cruel about my weight. I recall an occasion when I turned up at a school prom wearing a new dress. It had vertical stripes which, after reading a magazine article on the subject, I thought might help disguise my size. 'Hanna!' Stella shrieked from the other side of the room, 'is that a deckchair you're wearing?' prompting a collective laugh at my expense.

In spite of such incidents, I believed I was special to her and that she valued my friendship. I certainly worked hard at it: I would carry her bag to school, run errands for her and even do her homework (as I was much better at schoolwork than she was). Having received little emotional input from my parents, I did everything in my power to win her love and gratitude. Now I wonder whether it had been a waste of time. The thought that she might have been laughing at me behind my back is unbearable.

JC finishes his conversation and after replacing his mobile in his pocket, starts casting anxious glances at me. 'I'm sorry, Hanna,' he repeats, 'I shouldn't have said what I did.'

'No, you shouldn't have done.'

There's another awkward silence, then he says suddenly, 'I forgot to tell you, I saw her with that guy.'

'Who, Stella?'

'Yeah.'

'What guy? Hugh Whitmore?'

'No, that other smooth one she used to be with; Damian something or other.'

'Damian Matthews? But that was years ago.'

'Well, when I saw them together, it was shortly before her ...before she died.'

I'm startled. Stella never mentioned to me that she'd

been in contact with Damian. 'Where did you see them?'

'They were in a wine bar in Jubilee Street, deep in conversation. I saw them as I walked past one evening. I thought it was a bit odd. I knew they'd split up a long time ago.'

'Yes that does sound odd.' I wonder what business Stella could possibly have had with Damian Matthews after so many years.

'She didn't mention that she'd seen him?' JC asks.

'No, she didn't.' This is the second time I've been forced to admit that Stella didn't tell me she'd been in contact with a former partner, and when I think of how I comforted and supported her through her acrimonious break-ups with both Hugh and Damian, I'm filled with resentment. I wonder if I should mention what JC has told me to DI Forrester, or whether it would muddy the waters now that Hugh's been charged with Stella's murder.

Noticing that JC appears to be waiting for me to say something more, I change the subject to one I know is dear to his heart. 'How's the family, JC?'

He beams. 'Great, thanks for asking. Scarlett's in second year of secondary school and doing fine. She's got a leading role in the play they're doing at Christmas. Josh is nine. He's decided he's going to be a football pro. Did you know we've got a third sprog on the way? Sarah and I thought we'd completed our family, but...' he laughs. '...these things have a way of happening when you least expect it.'

I have difficulty reconciling the mischievous boy I remember from school with the responsible adult and proud parent sitting opposite me.

Before we separate, JC invites me to join him and his family for a meal one evening at their home. 'I'm sure Sarah and the kids would love to see you.'

I accept with pleasure, but as I make my way home, I can't stop thinking about what he has so tactlessly revealed – that Stella used to laugh at me behind my back. If what he told me is true – and I have no reason to believe that it isn't– what does it say about our friendship?

I first met Stella when we were both about five. She lived in the same road as me and went to the same primary school. She was the only child of older parents who adored her and gave her anything she set her heart on. Outside the home, her angelic blond beauty was constantly remarked upon and admired. As a result, she grew up with a strong sense of entitlement, convinced that others would always do what she wanted, which indeed was usually the case. At school where, to put it mildly, she didn't exactly shine, one pleading glance from those huge eyes was sufficient to make her teachers, especially the male ones, mark her efforts slightly higher than they actually merited.

With none of the same advantages in terms of parental devotion, looks and self-assurance, I was flattered that someone who inspired such universal adulation deigned to be friends with me, although this was probably only because we lived in such close proximity to each other and attended the same schools. My own family was of more modest means than Stella's, and while I envied her her smart clothes, the amount of pocket money she was given, and the lavish presents she received at Christmas and for birthdays, I believed that someone blessed with such amazing beauty deserved such rewards. I possibly also hoped – although I may not have been conscious of this at the time – that some of Stella's magic would rub off on me. And in a sense it did, in so far as being her closest friend (as I believed I was) gave me an entry into social circles both at school and outside that I never would have gained admittance to otherwise.

As the years passed, however, I became increasingly aware that I didn't like many of Stella's other friends. I didn't enjoy the kind of social environments she preferred either, but as I didn't want to relinquish the standing my connection with her bestowed on me, I continued to be her shadow and willing slave – a form of cowardice for which I now despise myself.

What was I to her? I ask myself now. Did she view me as her dogsbody rather than her friend – someone she could use, offload on, confide in? Maybe she only liked having me around because I was no competition, for Stella tended to regard other women as competition and couldn't bear to be upstaged. My lack of good looks probably made me a convenient foil for her beauty. Maybe she wasn't fond of me at all but took advantage of my constant help and support. It's painful to think this, but if it's true, I realise I only have myself to blame for allowing myself to be subservient to her for so long. The discovery that she may have repaid my devotion with mockery almost breaks my heart.

When I meet up with Maria in the evening I confide what JC told me about Stella.

'She was a bitch,' she declares succinctly.

This pulls me up short, causing me to re-evaluate my feelings and I'm filled with guilt. For so long my closest friend, surely Stella can't be reduced to a single negative word. Like the rest of us, she was complex: capable of both good and bad, generosity and meanness. In spite of what JC has told me, I must remember that in many ways she was a kind friend to me, inviting me to her home when we were children; taking me on holiday with her; lending me money to put down on a flat when I returned to Brighton.

'No,' I tell Maria, 'she wasn't a bitch, although she could be bitchy. She was my best friend.' But it strikes me now with the force of a revelation that there were occasions when I hated Stella almost as fiercely as I loved her. This is something I've never admitted to myself before.

My head is buzzing with these thoughts when I resume my work on the story about the girl and the elves. Disturbingly, I notice that the expression on Stella's face has subtly changed in my latest illustrations. She looks somewhat less innocent and angelic than in the earlier stages of the book.

# Chapter 15

Despite my doubts about the motive for Aidan's interest in me, I take particular care over my appearance before I go to meet him, and put on some of my new clothes. I have been feeling ridiculously nervous about spending time with him, but the evening turns out to be so enjoyable that I rapidly feel at ease in his company. To my relief he keeps off the subject of Stella and the party. Instead our conversation ranges over a variety of topics – local matters, items in the national news, the latest films and music events. Before we leave the pub, Aidan asks me about my work and expresses an interest in how I set about illustrating a book. 'Could you show me what you're doing some time?' he asks shyly.

Flattered, I ask him to visit me in my flat whenever he's passing.

I'm amazed when he calls round the following evening on his way home from work. I show him some of the books I've illustrated and explain the process involved – how I have to liaise with the graphic designers engaged by the publishers and send mock-ups which they then return with comments and suggestions. When I show him the work I've done so far on the story of the girl and the elves, he goes slightly pale and is momentarily silent.

'She…looks just like Stella,' he stutters eventually.

For some obscure reason I feel guilty. 'I know. It wasn't deliberate. It just happened. But once I'd drawn her the first time, I found I couldn't change the face, and since the author and designer are happy with what I've done so far, I've kept it. Now I see it as a kind of homage to her.'

He nods. 'Oh, I see.'

As he still looks rather shaken, I assume the pictures have stirred up unhappy memories and quickly put my work away.

A few days later he calls and asks me if I'd like to accompany him on Saturday morning on one of his favourite walks – along the sea path from Brighton Marina to Rottingdean. Surprised and pleased, I accept.

He calls for me at ten. It's a fine summer's day and the sunlight reflecting off the chalk cliffs is so dazzling that I need to put on sunglasses. After a period of unseasonably bad weather in July, the sun has encouraged crowds of people to come out to enjoy the sea air. As a result, our progress is frequently impeded by speeding cyclists and groups of walkers who selfishly straddle the entire width of the path. Some have dogs on long leads that wind around our legs and ankles.

We stop for coffee at a kiosk and while we drink it, I glance surreptitiously at Aidan.

I like the way his eyes disappear when he laughs and his nervous habit of pushing aside his fair hair when it flops onto his forehead. But I find one of the most attractive things about him is his speaking voice: a rich baritone with a slight Geordie lilt. Is it possible to fall in love with a voice? I believe it is.

I'm disconcerted when he suddenly launches, unprompted, into the story of his eight-year marriage and how his wife finally left him for someone else. 'I should have seen it coming,' he tells me glumly. 'Joanna used to say I was dull; boring! Maybe she was right, but I didn't fancy clubbing at our age, or spending all our leisure time in pubs or at gigs. It might have been different if we'd had kids, but she was adamant she didn't want any.' His voice shakes with sudden anger.

I hadn't solicited these confidences and don't know how to respond. I think it's a pity that neither of the two women Aidan fell in love with wanted children. Stella, like Joanna, also insisted she would never be a mother. I could never understand this view. I've always believed it would be wonderful to have a child; someone you could love unconditionally.

After coffee we stroll on to Saltdean and after pottering about on the beach, we have lunch at a café facing the sea. From our table on the terrace we watch children exploring rock pools and filling their small buckets with shingly sand. I'm mesmerised by the gleaming patterns the sun is creating on the surface of the water and decide that this is by far the most enjoyable day I've experienced in a very long time. The walk has acted as a welcome restorative to my low spirits and for the first time since I left hospital, I feel liberated from the melancholy thoughts that have haunted me since I was told the reason for my ending up there. And the more I see of him, the more I appreciate Aidan's company. He's an interesting companion with perceptive views on current affairs, both local and national and a sharp sense of irony I never noticed in the past. I've also discovered that he loves music – particularly classical music. He tells me that whatever he listens to remains imprinted on his mind and goes round endlessly in his head until another piece of music replaces it. An "earworm" he calls it. I often hear him humming fragments of the last piece he's heard. I find this habit endearing although I remember Stella telling me she found it intensely irritating. Like Joanna, Stella also used to say she thought Aidan was dull, which I interpreted as meaning he was too serious and intellectual for her. In my opinion he's anything *but* dull. It's unfortunate that he was attracted to the wrong women, just as she was always attracted to the wrong men. Now that I'm getting to know him better, it has become clear to me that had he and Stella ever got together as he so passionately desired, it would have been a disaster.

As if he can read my thoughts, Aidan comments, 'I once asked Stella to come on this walk with me. She laughed at me!'

It's my turn to laugh. 'Stella didn't "do" walks! She preferred going for drives in expensive cars.'

'I know,' he says ruefully. 'I sometimes invited her to come for drives as well, but she obviously didn't think my battered old Renault was up to scratch... Come to think of it, it *was* pretty scratched.' He gives a short laugh then gazes gloomily into the distance.

I feel a wave of sympathy for him, recalling the extent to which I allowed Stella to dictate my own leisure activities when we were younger. I used to tag along like a faithful dog when she frequented bars, clubs and other crowded environments where she would immediately become a magnet for male attention. Yet once again I have to accept that this was entirely my own fault: I was just as much in thrall to Stella as her admirers were. I agreed to accompany her to such places despite being fully aware that I would have derived far more pleasure from simpler activities such as the walk I'm enjoying now. I don't confide these thoughts to Aidan as he's so protective of Stella's memory.

He turns and smiles at me and my heart flips. With a flutter of excitement, I get the impression that I may be seeing a lot more of him in the future, for, astonishingly and against all expectation, he seems to be genuinely interested in *me*.

# Chapter 16

I spend a pleasant evening with JC and his wife, Sarah. Sarah is a small and pretty nurse in the early stages of her third pregnancy. Scarlett, their eldest child, has a round smiley face that resembles her father's, and Josh is small, intense and dark-haired like his mother. He has recently started learning the violin at school and before we start the meal, he decides to demonstrate his new skill to me by sawing vigorously at the open strings with the bow, making an excruciating screechy sound. The entertainment lasts for several uncomfortable minutes until he is gently requested to stop by his mother.

The family's two cats, Bubble and Squeak, follow us hopefully into the dining room but JC shoos them away.

Sarah serves pasta with a green salad, followed by poached pears with cream. It's a convivial meal and I have to suppress a pang of envy at the warm and cheerful family atmosphere – something I've never had the good fortune to experience myself.

After the children have been sent up to bed, JC, Sarah and I move into the living room where we continue to chat late into the night. We cover many topics and thankfully, neither of them broaches the subject of what happened to Stella and myself on the night of the party.

I discover that JC has a strong social conscience and is much exercised by the growing number of rough sleepers in the local area and elsewhere.

'British towns are turning into cardboard cities; we're becoming like a third world country,' he fulminates, rather red-faced after the number of beers he's consumed during the course of the evening (Sarah and I have stuck to wine). 'Did you know most of *Whitmore Future's* luxury flats are still empty?' he asks me.

I wince at the mention of Hugh's company. 'No, but I'm not surprised.'

'Nobody can afford to buy them – or rent them, come to that. And I hear construction's come to a halt on his latest development. There's a rumour he's been involved in some dodgy accounting.'

'That doesn't surprise me either.'

'And there are still unanswered questions about Regency Towers, that block of flats that started disintegrating a year or so ago. It beggars belief that he didn't know what the contractors were up to.'

I intercept a warning glance that Sarah flashes at him and infer from it that she's worried that references to Hugh will be painful to me. I'm touched by her sensitivity.

JC opens another can of beer and pours it into his glass before returning to his theme. 'It's about time the Government did something more than mouth platitudes and make empty promises about providing more affordable homes. Affordable homes my arse! Why's it possible for council tenants to buy their homes when there's such a dearth of social housing for people on low incomes? And don't start me on what's been happening with the NHS …and the chaos around leaving Europe--'

'Calm down, JC.' Sarah, who's sitting beside him on the sofa, reaches up and pats him affectionately on the cheek. 'I'm sure Hanna shares your concerns.'

'I do,' I say hastily. 'You're right; what's happening is really worrying, but I'm afraid I've had other things on my mind lately.'

JC looks ashamed. 'Sorry, Hanna, you shouldn't have to listen to me pontificating after what you've been through.'

Sarah glances at him with a slight shake of her head, from which I deduce that they had jointly agreed not to allude to what happened to Stella and myself. Checking my watch, I see that it's nearly half past midnight and decide it's time to go home.

\* \* \*

When I return to the neurological unit for a check-up with the consultant, she asks whether I've been suffering from any of the problems listed in the booklet I was given on my discharge from hospital. I tell her I'm still plagued by anxiety and headaches and have occasional emotional meltdowns.

She nods and tells me this is to be expected after a traumatic brain injury and when I complain that I still can't remember what happened on the night of the party, she tries to reassure me. 'Give it time, Hanna. Stop worrying about it. Relax! Trying too hard to remember could be counterproductive. If your memory is going to return, it will do so in its own good time, probably when you least expect it.'

I describe to her the recurrent nightmare I have about a man standing over Stella's blood-streaked body. She says this isn't surprising in the circumstances, and if necessary, I should ask my GP to prescribe antidepressants. Overall, however, she seems pleased with my progress and suggests I contact one of the support groups that have been established for people who have suffered head injuries. Although I tell her I will, I know I probably won't. I fear I might become too preoccupied with the possible long-term effects of what has happened to me.

I don't mention that, as well as the nightmares, I sometimes dream that Stella's still alive and that we're young women again. In most of the dreams Stella is characteristically flirting with a bevy of admirers and I'm hovering, as usual, on the periphery of the group. But in one of them, I'm walking a few steps behind her and someone else – a man whose back looks familiar. The two of them are hand in hand and engaged in intimate conversation. Stella suddenly glances at me over her shoulder and laughs in a sneering sort of way. When her companion turns, I realise with a sense of shock, that it's Aidan. The dream left me with an uneasy feeling that clung to me for the rest of the day.

Since the walk to Saltdean, I've actually been seeing a lot of Aidan. We now meet once or twice a week, usually at his suggestion, for a drink or a meal. Sometimes we go for a long country walk at weekends; occasionally we go to a film or concert or visit a museum. He's a stimulating companion who is widening my intellectual horizons considerably, particularly where classical music is concerned; something I was never interested in before but am now beginning to appreciate.

He is also very thoughtful: gentle, kind and solicitous about my health. When I'm with him I feel safe; protected. But despite our growing friendship, we're not yet what might be called "an item". Apart from a kiss on the cheek when we meet and part, and an occasional casual arm around my shoulders, he hasn't attempted to go any further, and although I feel more attracted to him than ever, in a way I'm relieved. I don't feel ready for any more emotional upheavals just yet, and I suspect Aidan doesn't either. For all his complaints about her, he's probably still missing his ex wife. And although I know he likes me and seems to enjoy my company, I don't think he's physically attracted to me, at least not in the same overwhelming way he was attracted to Stella.

# Chapter 17

When I go out, I occasionally have an uneasy feeling that I'm being watched – that instinct you sometimes have that somebody's eyes are on you even when the owner of them isn't actually in your line of vision. But although I turn round frequently, I never spot anyone. Sometimes my phone rings and when I answer it, no-one speaks and the number is unavailable. I try not to panic as it could just be one of those irritating cold calls. I'm reluctant to mention these incidents to the police as I don't want them to think I'm being paranoid, but I can't help feeling a little scared. When a complete stranger contacts me through my website and asks if we can meet to discuss a possible commission, I'm immediately suspicious and arrange to meet him in a busy Brighton café. He turns out to be a perfectly legitimate author who wants me to illustrate one of his books. I try to persuade myself that now Hugh is in custody, my fears are irrational and just another after-effect of the head injury. And as the days pass, they diminish, until…

One night, after I've been to the nearest supermarket to get some grocery items I've run out of, I'm walking home along an empty road when I hear footsteps in the distance behind me that appear to be keeping pace with mine. Although it's not particularly late, it's already dark. When I start to speed up, so do the footsteps. My heart starts to pound painfully, but I don't turn round or start to run as I don't want to betray my growing panic. As the footsteps draw closer, I feel prickles of fear down my back. Grabbing my keys from my pocket – the only items I have with me that could serve as a potential weapon – I veer away from the dark doorways on my left and cross into the middle of the road.

'Hanna?'

Did someone call my name or was it my imagination?

For a fraction of a second I freeze, totally panicked, then adrenalin kicks in. I break into a run and sprint towards the corner. Before I turn into my road, I glance back and glimpse a tall male figure less than a hundred yards behind me. Reaching the block where I live, I scurry through the outer doors, unlock the inner ones and almost fall inside. Fortunately the entrance to the building is secure enough to deter unauthorised visitors, so even if he's seen which building I entered, he won't be able to follow.

Safely in the foyer, I drop my bag of groceries and lean against the wall panting with exertion. When I've recovered my breath, I pick up the shopping and climb shakily up to the first floor and bang on Maria's door.

'Whatever's the matter, Hanna?' she exclaims when she opens it. 'You're as white as a sheet.'

After I describe what has happened, she urges me to call the police.

'I will but I've left my phone in the flat.'

'You can use mine.' She offers me her mobile.

'I can't. The detective's number won't be on it. I'll have to ring him on mine.'

As soon as I enter my flat, I call DI Forrester and leave a

message asking him to call me back.

There's no response. In fact I don't hear from him until the next morning, after I've spent a restless, almost sleepless night. He apologises for the delay, explaining that he was off duty and attending a social function. When I tell him about the man following me, he clucks his tongue.

'Did you see what he looked like?'

'I only caught a glimpse – tall, quite thickset.'

'But you didn't recognise him?'

'No, it was too dark.'

'But he called your name?'

'I think so.'

'Did you recognise the voice?'

'No, he wasn't near enough.'

'Well, it was obviously someone who knows you if he called your name.'

'I suppose so, but I was too scared to stop and find out who he was.' I feel embarrassed for he must think I'm being paranoid.

'If anything like this happens again,' the detective advises me, 'ring me at once and we'll send someone to check around the area. Don't give your address and phone number to anyone unless you trust them.'

I'm not reassured. 'Do you think it could have something to do with what happened to Stella?'

'I shouldn't think so,' he tells me. 'As you know, Whitmore's been charged with the murder. But if you're worried about anyone following you again, or if you have any suspicious phone calls, let me know.'

For a while I feel too nervous to go out on my own after dark, but nothing else happens to disturb my peace of mind and I try to put the incident out of my mind.

# Chapter 18

I haven't experienced any more scary incidents and am feeling much calmer, but I'm still slightly nervous about going out at night alone. As a result, Maria and I have now established a pattern of eating out together one evening every fortnight, each of us choosing the restaurant in turn. This week we go for an Italian meal, which is my choice. (I make a point of avoiding the places I used to frequent with Stella).

We're enjoying our meal when with a jolt of shock, I spot Damian Matthews, Stella's obnoxious former partner with the gambling addiction. He's sitting a few tables away with a woman, an attractive fair-haired one (though not in Stella's league). I hope he hasn't noticed me and that if he looks my way, he won't recognise me. I know – and a number of people have told me – that I look rather different from how I used to. I've kept my hair short and recently had it tinted a chestnut shade which seems to suit me. Damian looks much the same, although I notice that he's stockier than in the past and his ginger hair has faded to a kind of sandy grey. Spotting him glancing my way, I quickly avert my gaze.

Maria and I are half way through our meal when out of the corner of my eye I see Damian and his companion rise from their table as if about to leave the restaurant. Instead of heading for the door, however, he stops, mutters something to the woman he's with, then makes his way across the floor to where Maria and I are sitting.

'Hanna? It *is* you? I wasn't sure. At first I thought it was someone who looked like you.'

'Yes, it is me,' I mutter coldly. I notice he's dressed very smartly and wonder whether he's finally won at cards.

He glances at Maria then back at me. 'You look… different.'

I don't answer and don't introduce him to Maria.

He clears his throat. 'I was very sorry to hear about…I mean …you know--'

I cut him off before he can say any more. 'Are you still living in Brighton?'

He seems relieved at the change of subject. 'No, I moved to Wimbledon a long time ago but I'm working on a project here at the moment so I rent a room in Hove during the week and go home at weekends. You still live in Brighton?'

'Yes. But not where I used to.'

'Well I must say you're looking fantastic, Hanna; transformed!' He smiles winningly at me, reminding me of how he could always turn on the charm. And I notice he still has those sleepy "come to bed" eyes that seduced Stella some years ago.

'Perhaps we could meet and have a chat some time?' he adds.

I'm incredulous. Why on earth would Damian Matthews want to have "a chat" with me? When he and Stella were together, it was clear how much we disliked each other and I haven't forgotten how badly he behaved after she left him. Before I can think of a suitable reply, however,

I hear his name being called. His companion, standing by the restaurant door, is displaying signs of impatience and staring at me with undisguised hostility.

'My wife's waiting, I'd better go.' Damian gives a false-sounding laugh. 'She's come to join me for a few days to check on what I'm getting up to!' He regards me hesitantly and when I don't respond, mutters, 'Cheers, then. It was nice seeing you again, Hanna.' After another uncertain glance at me, he ambles off to join his wife.

'Who was that?' Maria asks.

'One of Stella's old flames. I can't stand him. That's why I didn't introduce you.'

'Ah.' Maria nods. She's heard enough about Stella's disastrous liaisons from me to understand.

I quickly forget about Damian Matthews, but one morning when I'm about to pop out to do some shopping, I'm amazed to find him standing at the outer door of the building, studying the numbers of the flats listed beside the intercom. Before I can escape back inside, he accosts me.

'I'm glad I've seen you, Hanna. I heard you lived here but didn't know which flat was yours.'

'What do you want?' I mutter ungraciously. 'I'm in a hurry.'

'Just a few words. There's something I'd like to ask you.'

'What?' I hope he doesn't want to talk about Stella and wonder whether he'll mention that he was in touch with her before she was murdered.

'It's...' he glances around. 'Erm, would you mind if we went somewhere quiet for a minute? It's not something I want to talk about here.'

'I'd rather not.'

'Please, I promise I won't take up much of your time.'

'Five minutes then.' Curious in spite of myself, I accompany him to the nearest café where he buys us both coffees.

'What's this about?' I ask him curtly.

'Hugh Whitmore.'

My heart sinks. 'What about him?'

'I've heard he's in custody, charged with Stella's murder.'

'What about it?'

He hesitates. 'I've been working in Brighton and Hove on and off for the last few months, making a documentary about all the building developments that have been springing up in the city.'

'You mean *Whitmore Futures* developments?'

'Yes, as it happens, a lot of them *are* WF developments.'

'And?'

'In the course of my research for the piece, I managed to gain access to some of the people who worked for Whitmore. One of them told me... things.'

'What sort of "things"?'

Damian takes two sugar lumps from a bowl and drops them into his cup. 'Apparently he's been purchasing cheap, substandard materials and claiming they meet planning and fire regulations; not paying his suppliers; supplying false information to the auditors. The list goes on and on.'

'So?' Nothing would surprise me about Hugh Whitmore, but I wonder why Damian is telling me this.

'Remember the collapse of Regency Towers?' he continues.

'Of course I do!' Regency Towers, one of Hugh's most notorious developments, was a large and, in my opinion, extremely ugly block of flats that started to develop ominous cracks in the concrete cladding only a few years after its erection. Fortunately the building was evacuated before anything worse happened. It was rapidly made safe and fenced off, but has been abandoned ever since and remains a local eyesore – a magnet for graffiti-artists and fly-tippers. No-one seems to know if or when it will be demolished.

Damian stirs his tea vigorously. 'According to my source, the disaster was entirely due to Whitmore's negligence. He'd been cutting corners as usual. But at the enquiry, he blamed the contractors; said they'd employed dodgy subcontractors and unskilled labourers from abroad who'd ignored planning requirements and used the wrong materials without his knowledge, then buggered off back to Poland or wherever, after they'd been paid. If you can believe that! Obviously it was up to him to perform due diligence on the contractors and subcontractors, but to cut a long story short, he escaped prosecution and they got the flak. What a travesty! He got away with it.'

I laugh. 'That doesn't surprise me. Hugh usually got away with everything.' (Though *not* with murder, I think to myself).

'Yeah,' Damian mutters, 'it's gotta be because the guy's a Mason… funny handshakes and all that; know what I mean?'

'No, not really.'

'Well it's well established that he was in cahoots with Robertson.'

'Robertson?'

'Yeah, Ian Robertson, Chair of the Planning Committee. He always made sure Whitmore developments were nodded through.'

'Did he?' I wonder if this was the reason for Aidan's surprise that the Robertsons had been invited to Stella's party. 'I don't know anything about that, but if it was a disgruntled employee who told you, couldn't it just be grudge talk?'

'Possibly,' Damian taps his cup impatiently with the teaspoon. 'But it confirmed what a number of other people I interviewed have been claiming, or insinuating, about the way Whitmore runs his business. From what they told me, it seems clear that he was entirely responsible for the Regency Towers disaster. As the owner of the freehold, it was up to him to arrange insurance for the property as a whole, but his insurers are refusing to pay any compensation. They're claiming non-compliance because he didn't comply with the conditions of the policy. Although he blamed the contractors for what happened, they insist that he must have given them specifications regarding the materials they used.' Damian takes a gulp of his tea and bangs his cup down on the table. 'The poor buggers who bought or rented flats in Regency Towers have been left high and dry.'

'Yes, I believe I heard something to that effect.' I still wonder why Damian is telling me this.

'Apparently someone who'd bought the luxury penthouse in the Towers went and confronted Whitmore in his office. It would have come to fisticuffs if the staff hadn't got between them and ejected him.'

I'm rather sorry to hear that the disgruntled flat-owner didn't manage to bop Hugh on the nose! 'Did your source tell the Regency Towers enquiry what he knew?'

'No, and it was a she. I imagine Whitmore either threatened her or bought her off.'

'Well, what about you? Have you told anyone?'

He hesitates and glances quickly around before

muttering, 'Only Stella.'

I'm flabbergasted. 'You told *Stella*?'

'Yes, you knew that didn't you?'

'I had no idea.'

'No?' He stares at me with an air of surprise.

'When did you tell her?'

'Not that long ago; a month or so before she was … before she died.'

'She must have been taken aback to hear from *you* after all this time.' I can't suppress the sarcasm in my voice.

'She was.' He looks uncomfortable. 'Look, it wasn't my choice to split up. You know that, Hanna. I was devastated when she left me.'

'Were you?' I mutter sceptically, still wondering where all this is heading. 'Why did you decide to tell Stella of all people what you heard about Regency Towers?'

'I needed more information for the project; I thought if anyone knew about the kind of stuff Whitmore was up to, it would be her.'

'And did she know what he was up to?'

'She told me she was aware he was involved in some dodgy accounting but said she didn't know he was responsible for the Regency Towers collapse.' He pauses and lowers his voice. 'It was when I told her about it that she suggested we got Whitmore to pay us to keep quiet.'

I almost drop my cup. 'She *what*? Are you saying Stella suggested *blackmailing* Hugh?'

He gives me an odd look. 'You mean you didn't know?'

'No I didn't know, and I don't believe you.'

He laughs. 'Come off it, Hanna! You must have known darling Stella wasn't averse to getting back at the bastard for the way he tried to stint on the divorce settlement, and presumably for stuff that went on during the marriage.'

I swallow hard. 'Of course I knew she had every reason to be angry with him; to hate him; but she would never have contemplated *blackmailing* him. Why are you telling me this?'

His expression changes to one of astonishment. 'You *are* kidding me, aren't you? You *must* have known about it.'

'Why would I?'

'You and Stella were both so close, I assumed she confided in you about everything.'

'Obviously not.' A surge of hot anger courses through me, but I'm not sure whether it's towards him or towards Stella. 'Do the police know about this? It's obviously relevant to the murder investigation.'

He glances uncertainly at me. 'I thought Whitmore might have mentioned it to them himself by now.'

I give an incredulous laugh. 'He's been charged with murder, for God's sake. He's hardly likely to have told the police that he was responsible for criminal negligence as well! More to the point, why haven't *you* told the police? If Stella *was* threatening to blackmail Hugh, it proves he had a motive to...do what they think he did.'

Damian moves his chair uncomfortably close to mine and whispers, 'I haven't told them because she told me she asked Whitmore to cough up fifty K to keep her quiet...' he glances again at me '... and she was going to give me half.'

'*What?*'

He looks shamefaced. 'I needed the cash. I had bad gambling debts and Stella was keen for me to expose as much bad stuff about Whitmore as possible in my documentary, so I said I would in exchange for the money. But things never got that far. She told me she was expecting him to bring her the cash that weekend – the weekend she died, but I don't know whether he did or not. I was at home in Wimbledon at the time and I never heard from her again …for obvious reasons.' He gulps. 'Maybe he decided to kill her rather than hand over fifty grand.'

I catch my breath. If what Damian's telling me is true, then Hugh must have gone to Stella's flat that night not because she was the "love of his life" as he claimed to the police, but either to pay her to keep quiet about his role in the Regency Towers catastrophe, or to silence her forever. On balance the second scenario seems the more plausible of the two. DI Forrester has never mentioned finding a large sum of money in Stella's flat, although he's so circumspect in what he tells me, maybe that isn't surprising.

'Hanna?' Uncharacteristically, Damian is stammering. 'Do you know whether Whitmore gave Stella the money or not?'

I'm surprised at the question. 'Why would I know that?'

'Because you were there that night when she was murdered. You were there when Whitmore went to the flat.'

'How do you know I was there?'

He laughs sarcastically. 'Pull the other one! I heard you were found with head injuries. It's obvious what happened: you knew what was going on and that's why Whitmore attacked you after he killed Stella.'

I start to shake with anger. 'I've already told you, I wasn't aware of any blackmail plan. And if Hugh did go to the flat intending to kill Stella, he was hardly likely to take fifty grand with him, was he?'

'You tell me! You're the most likely person to know.' Damian thrusts his face close to mine. 'What have you told the police, Hanna? Tell me. Do they know I was involved?'

I rise to my feet, pushing back my chair. 'I haven't said anything to the police because this is the first time I've heard this story. And if you don't go and tell them exactly what you've just told me, *I* will. Don't contact me again.'

His face darkens. 'I always thought you were a fucking hard bitch.'

I nearly retaliate with some choice words that could apply to him, but think better of it and stalk out of the café.

Instead of performing the errand that had brought me out in the first place, I return home in a state of agitation. The idea that Stella would be mixed up in something as sordid as blackmail, let alone be the instigator of it, is horrifying. Although I can understand her resentment towards Hugh, I find it difficult to believe she would be guilty of such a thing, especially as her recent phone exchanges with him apparently implied to the police that the two of them were back on friendly terms (although I still consider that to be highly unlikely). Could she have been tempted by the prospect of such a large sum of money? That also seems unlikely. I know Stella loved luxury but she certainly wasn't hard up following the divorce settlement and always seemed to have enough to spend on designer clothes, holidays and social occasions. Moreover she knew that her parents would help her financially if she ever fell on hard times. She was their only heir, and I remember her telling me that they sent her money on a regular basis to reduce the amount of inheritance tax payable on their estate after they passed away.

No, she certainly didn't need the money, so what was she thinking of? But…the idea suddenly occurs to me – what if it was *Damian* who instigated the blackmail plot? This seems far more plausible than his claim that it was Stella who suggested it. It would of course be very convenient for him to shift the blame onto someone who will never be in a position to contradict his story.

# Chapter 19

A few days after my encounter with Damian, DI Forrester calls round. I make him coffee and we take our mugs into the living room.

'Damian Matthews has come out of the woodwork,' the detective announces abruptly after settling into an armchair and making the usual polite enquiries about my health. 'He's come forward with some information relevant to the murder investigation. Did you know he was back in town?'

'Yes, he came round to see me a couple of days ago.' I'm relieved to hear that Damian has spoken to the police, although I suspect he may have played down his own role in the attempt to extort money from Hugh.

The detective's thick eyebrows rise until they almost join his hairline. 'And you didn't think to mention this to me?'

'I thought it would be better if he spoke to you himself. I advised him to tell the police what he told me.'

'And what was that?'

I paraphrase Damian's revelations about Regency Towers and the alleged blackmail plan.

DI Forrester frowns. 'That's basically the story he told us. I gather he's making some sort of film documentary about recent planning developments in Brighton and Hove.'

'Do you believe what he said, about the blackmail?'

He tuts. 'Nasty business, blackmail. We assume that what Matthews has told us is true since Whitmore has now admitted that it is, although, perhaps unsurprisingly, he didn't mention it before. The evidence is certainly stacking up against him. It means the prosecution will have a stronger case when he goes for trial.' He glances at me. 'It appears your friend Stella wasn't exactly…lily white, was she?'

I'm silent.

The detective takes a sip from his mug then puts it gently down on the coaster I've provided on the coffee table. He fixes me with a searching look. 'Were you aware that Stella was threatening Whitmore with blackmail, Hanna?'

'N-no, of course I wasn't!' Indignation makes me stutter. 'I can't believe she was capable of anything like that. It's inconceivable.'

He makes no comment but his continuing steady gaze makes me feel uncomfortable.

'What if it was *Damian* who thought the whole thing up, not Stella?' I suggest. 'He told me he had bad gambling debts. Isn't it possible that he proposed the idea of extorting money from Hugh to Stella when he contacted her to find out what she knew about Regency Towers?'

The detective shakes his head. 'There's no evidence that Matthews was the one to instigate the plan. In fact Whitmore wasn't even aware of his involvement. As far as he was concerned, the threat came from Stella alone. She didn't tell him who gave her the information about Regency Towers.'

My heart sinks. 'Well if it's true, I hope her parents never get to hear of it. It would be a terrible shock for them on top of everything else.'

'Indeed.' He retrieves his mug and takes another sip of

his coffee.

'But it doesn't make sense.'

'What doesn't?'

'You told me the phone exchanges between Stella and Hugh were friendly. You said he claimed she was thinking of getting back with him.'

'The messages *were* quite friendly in tone. There was absolutely nothing in them to suggest that Stella was blackmailing him. She was clever enough not to leave any threats or demands in any of them. When we first questioned Whitmore, he told us that the two of them met together twice before the party, at her request. Now he says he believes she was only *pretending* to be on more amicable terms with him, and he fell for it before discovering she was intending to put the boot in. He claims she threatened him with blackmail on the second occasion they met, about a week before the party.'

'But what about the pendant? Why would he have bothered to buy her an expensive birthday present if she was expecting him to hand over fifty thousand pounds?'

The detective gives a sceptical laugh. 'Good question! He claims he bought the pendant *before* she mentioned blackmailing him, and decided to give it to her in an attempt to try and charm her; talk her out of it.'

'That sounds pretty far-fetched to me.'

'And to me, although he says he never intended to give her the money. As the enquiry into Regency Towers had already exonerated him, he didn't think she could be serious. He thought she was bluffing.'

'And when he discovered she wasn't?'

The detective smiles grimly. 'He put the knife in, literally.'

I wince. 'But still claims he didn't?'

'Yes.'

'And the pendant still hasn't turned up?'

'No.'

'Do you think the story about the pendant is a fiction?'

'He showed us the receipt and the shop confirms that he bought it, but that doesn't prove that he actually gave it to Stella, so that part of the story could well be a fiction. The pendant is probably an irrelevance now in any case. Damian Matthews has supplied some of the evidence we need to justify the murder charge.'

'So what will happen to Damian?' I ask.

'Nothing. Both his and Whitmore's accounts indicate that the blackmail idea originated with Stella, and we have no concrete evidence of his involvement. It might be possible to bring a charge of criminal conspiracy against him as he admits he was willing to go along with the plan, but since we have no evidence that he took any action to further it and no money seems to have changed hands, it would be difficult to construct a case. So he's just been given a warning.'

I'm sorry to hear that Damian is escaping some of the blame. 'Well what about Hugh's role in the collapse of Regency Towers? It sounds as though he was entirely responsible for the building's collapse. Couldn't he be charged with criminal negligence as well as murder?'

The detective sighs. 'It was a nasty business, Regency Towers, very nasty, but my team is only concerned with the murder case. The irregularities in Whitmore's business practices are irrelevant unless we can prove that they contributed to his motive for killing Stella.' He glances at me with an enigmatic smile. 'While we're on the subject of

Regency Towers, you might be interested in hearing who bought the top floor flat there – the penthouse.'

'Who?'

'Steve Cottram.'

I'm astounded. 'Steve *Cottram*?'

'Yes…yet another of Stella's former lovers. It's a small world as they say. He was living there with some woman, but like the other occupants of the building, they had to move out when things started to go wrong with the building. No friend of Whitmore's apparently! He'd spent rather a lot of money on getting the penthouse done up just as he wanted it. He's taking legal action against the company.'

I shrug. 'As far as I'm concerned, he and Hugh are two of a kind. I haven't seen or heard from Steve for years, not since he and Stella split up.'

He gives me an odd look. 'Well *you* may not have heard from him for years, but Stella certainly had, and not that long before she died.'

'What?' My capacity for surprise is constantly being tested.

'There was an exchange of messages between them on Stella's mobile.'

'You mean they were still in touch, after all these years?'

'They apparently had several recent communications. You didn't know about that?'

'I had absolutely no idea. She never mentioned anything about it to me.' Once again I'm stunned at how much Stella had been concealing from me.

'Then it seems there was rather a lot your *close* friend didn't tell you.'

I feel my face go red. 'Have you spoken to Steve

Cottram?'

'Yes; he said he contacted Stella shortly before the birthday party. He got in touch with her, just as Matthews did, to try to find out how much she knew about Whitmore's company and his responsibility for the collapse of Regency Towers. He was hoping she might dish the dirt on his business practices to help him pursue his claim.' He drains his mug of coffee and replaces it on the coffee table. 'Strange how so many of Stella's former lovers were kind of …circling around her before she died, isn't it?' He checks his watch and rises to his feet.

'Yes, I suppose it is strange.' I stand up in my turn. 'It's as if they couldn't keep away from her. I don't know which one of them I disliked most. Stella kept going for the same type of man.'

'Unfortunately that seems to be a pattern with some women.'

I accompany the detective to the door. Reflecting on his final words, it strikes me that Stella was only attracted to men who were like her; men with an exaggerated sense of entitlement who expected to get what they wanted and became aggressive when other people didn't act in the way they desired. I recall how Stella herself behaved on the occasions when her wishes were thwarted, turning from wheedling to self-pity and ultimately, to spitefulness. I observed this throughout our long friendship but without judgment. Whenever she was in conflict with anyone, I usually wanted her to gain the upper hand whatever the rights and wrongs of the matter. I wonder now what that says about me.

# Chapter 20

I'm too preoccupied with the detective's latest revelations to resume work on my illustrations. What had Stella been playing at, agreeing to meet the men she'd fled from, complained about, wept over? And why – I ask myself again – why hadn't she *told* me they'd been in touch with her, especially after I'd supported her through the bitter break-ups with each one of them? I thought we were *friends*! My sense of grievance increases and I pace agitatedly around my flat until the need to replenish some of my art supplies provides me with an excuse to go out and clear my head.

I'm so immersed in my resentful thoughts as I make my way to the shop in Hove, that I fail to look where I'm going. I stumble over a figure lying in a sleeping bag on the pavement and drop my purse. A woman coming in the opposite direction grabs my hand and helps me regain my footing. 'Bloody nuisance, these people!' she mutters.

I look down at the obstacle that has tripped me up but the person at my feet doesn't move. A member of the growing army of homeless people that has taken up residence in the commercial areas of Brighton and Hove, he appears to be asleep. The only visible part of him is his head, supported on a backpack. It reveals him to be a man with wiry black hair, dark skin and a lot of facial stubble. There's a pair of scuffed shoes a few inches from his nose and a stack of bags and bundles under the shop window behind him. His long legs in the grubby sleeping bag protrude at an angle across the pavement, threatening to trip up other pedestrians.

As I bend to pick up my purse, the man opens his eyes and peers up at me. 'Yeah?' he mutters hoarsely.

'You're creating an obstacle on the pavement,' I tell him severely. 'You nearly made me fall over.'

'Oh, sorry.' He yawns then slowly rolls onto his side and levers himself out of the sleeping bag. Stiffly pulling himself upright, he thrusts his feet into the shoes then kicks his bed behind him. He's taller than me with a thin, rather drawn face, and looks as though he might be in his late twenties or early thirties.

Feeling guilty at my initial lack of charitable feelings, I fumble in my purse to find some change.

'No, you don't need to give me anything.' he says with an air of embarrassment. ' I'm not a...I mean, I'm not going to be here for long; it's only temporary, just till I'm back on my feet.'

'Oh.' I'm surprised he's so well spoken then immediately feel guilty again. Why shouldn't he be well spoken? I castigate myself for the automatic prejudice. But I've never known how to react to rough sleepers and whether to give them money or not, as people often tell me it might go on drugs or alcohol. But if I was forced to sleep on the streets, wouldn't *I* turn to drugs and alcohol?

I hold the coins I'd intended to give him uncertainly in my hand. 'Can I get you something to eat, then? A sandwich?'

Without looking at me, he mumbles, 'Thanks' and

squats down to tie his shoelaces.

I hurry to the nearest supermarket and purchase a chicken and salad sandwich and a can of *Coca Cola*. When I return I find him sitting on top of the sleeping bag with his knees drawn up to his chest. 'Thanks,' he repeats as I hand him the drink and sandwich.

I hover in front of him for a second, feeling I ought to initiate a conversation or at least express an interest in his plight, but I'm reluctant to appear patronising or too inquisitive. 'How --?' I begin to ask.

'How long have I been sleeping rough? About three weeks.' He tugs at the ring pull of the can of drink until it folds back with a hiss. Raising the can to his mouth, he takes a long draught of the contents.

'No, I mean how did it happen, the rough sleeping?' As the question comes out, I realise I probably *am* being too inquisitive.

'Long story.' He puts the can on the pavement beside him and starts to wrestle with the cellophane wrapping of the sandwich. He gives me a quizzical look. 'Are you *really* interested?'

'Yes.'

'Well, me and Alison, my girl friend... my *former* girl friend, that is, we used to rent a flat in Regency Towers...'

'Regency Towers?' My interest is piqued.

'Yeah, you know, that rubbish block that started to disintegrate? Whoever designed that monstrosity should be shot! We rented one of those poky flats on the ground floor, the ones earmarked for the hoi polloi. When bits started dropping off the outside, all the people living in the block were evacuated. Me and Ali were put up in a crap B and B. We had a crummy basement room. We were told it was only temporary but we ended up being stuck there for over a year.'

'That must have been tough.' As I speak I realise what a stupid understatement this is.

'Yeah! Tough's the word. We weren't offered anything else and couldn't find a flat we could afford. It was fucking cramped with the two of us living in one room and we started getting on each other's nerves.' Having finally succeeded in releasing the sandwich from the wrapper, he takes a large bite out of one of the halves.

I wait for him to continue.

'Still interested?' he asks when he's finished chewing.

'Yes.'

'Ali said she'd had enough and buggered off back to London to stay with a friend.'

'What did you do after she'd gone?'

'I couldn't afford to stay in the B and B for long on my own, so I did a spot of sofa-surfing. But you can only go on doing that for so long. The last time I kipped on a mate's couch, his girl friend got pissed off with me being there every night, and by then I'd exhausted all other options, so …' he gives a twisted grin. 'There you have it. That's why I ended up here.'

'No family?' One again I fear I'm being too intrusive.

He shrugs. 'They're in Manchester, what's left of them: just my mum, stepfather and a married sister with two kids.'

'Don't you have a job? Haven't you been earning?'

'You ask a lot of questions!' He takes another bite of the sandwich and munches slowly. 'I *had* a job, at least I had a half decent one when me and Ali were together. I was working at Marlows - remember the electronics firm that went bust about three months ago?' He gives a bitter laugh.

'Great timing, don't you think? After that, I got a job in a coffee bar to tide me over while I was looking for somewhere else to live. But you know the kind of rents you have to pay here? I couldn't find anything for under a grand a month, not even for nasty council flats that'd been bought by previous tenants, and I just wasn't earning enough. It's not just the rent you have to find: they expect you to stump up for a bunch of additional things before you can even get a sniff at a place. It was hopeless. And it wasn't just the money that was a problem. One estate agent told me that some landlords won't rent to me because of what I look like. They think they'd have to check on my immigration status!' He gives an outraged laugh. '*Immigration* status? I was born in Manchester, for God's sake! My dad came over with the Windrush generation and my mum's English.'

I'm appalled. 'That's awful.'

'I can think of better words to describe it!' he swallows the rest of the *Coca Cola* and puts the empty can on the pavement next to him.

'So how did you--?'

He utters a theatrical sigh. 'You really want to hear the rest?'

'Yes.'

'Well, I was advised my best bet would be to find a room in a shared house and I'd just started looking for one, when I lost the coffee bar job. I got there late a few times in the mornings a couple of weeks ago. It was just after I started sleeping rough. It was so cold, I stayed awake most of the night and didn't drop off until about five in the morning, then didn't wake up in time. So they told me to go.' He picks up the empty can and crushes it violently in his fist. 'And before you ask, I've been to the council housing office umpteen times, but they say I'm not in the "Priority Need" group. They put me in touch with an outreach team, St Mungos. They come round with hot drinks and stuff, and tell you where homeless shelters are. I did go to a hostel for a few nights, but there were some guys shouting and fighting there during the night – rough types; druggies… I got abuse too … racist crap, so I thought I'd be safer out here.'

I feel overwhelmed with sympathy for him. 'Can't you apply for benefits?'

'I did…I do, but it's a constant struggle. To claim JSA – that's Job Seekers' Allowance in case you don't know – you need to have a full-time address and to be actively trying to get work. I've tried looking for another job, but I can't afford to keep topping up my phone let alone pay for bus fares to get to work interviews and the Job Centre every two weeks to sign on. To cut a long story short, they cut off my JSA because I couldn't supply enough proof that I was looking for work.' His mouth twitches. 'You're trapped every which way. You just can't win.'

I can't think of anything to say.

He munches gloomily on the rest of the sandwich, then looks up at me. 'I'm Robbie, by the way. Robbie Cole.'

'Hanna,' I respond. 'Hanna Walker.' I shuffle my feet, embarrassed at not being able to think of anything that would be remotely helpful. 'I'd better get going.'

He smiles at me revealing even white teeth and his face is transformed. 'Cheers, Hanna, and thanks again for the sandwich.'

As I continue on my way to the art suppliers, angry thoughts race through my head. The poor guy's misfortunes were entirely due to the collapse of Regency Towers. Hugh Whitmore has more than murder to answer for!

When JC and Sarah come round to my flat for a return meal, I describe my encounter with Robbie Cole. 'I felt really sorry for him,' I tell them. 'Everything seems to have conspired against him finding a job and somewhere to live.'

JC looks grim. 'There are too many landlords charging outrageous rents these days and too many Whitmores. People like him are taking advantage of the housing crisis to erect substandard accommodation.'

Maria, who has joined us for the evening, agrees. 'A lot of the students I teach are amazed to see so many people sleeping on the streets here. They thought Britain was a prosperous country.'

JC frowns. 'I've read that some London boroughs are giving rough sleepers the money for train fares so that they can get rid of the problem of people sleeping on *their* streets.'

Maria tells us a story she read in a local paper, about a homeless man who'd been keeping his possessions in a wheelie bin which he pushed from one place to another. 'Then the inevitable happened.'

'What was that?' asks JC.

'When he went for a pee, the binmen passed on their rounds and they emptied his wheelie bin.'

We greet the story with mingled groans and laughs.

Sarah comes in from the hall where she's been calling the babysitter to make sure all is well at home. She looks blooming in her fifth month of pregnancy and I feel a twinge of envy. 'Young people have a tough time these days,' she says, catching the gist of our conversation. 'I wonder what kind of future *our* kids'll have when they grow up. Maybe they'll end up of the streets too through no fault of their own.'

JC looks appalled. 'I bloody well hope they don't!'

'Well you never know. If that young man Hanna met fell on hard times so quickly, it could happen to anyone; and who's to say where our children will be when they're adults or what they'll be doing? They won't necessarily be on our doorstep where we can help.'

The conversation has taken a rather gloomy turn so I try to lighten the atmosphere by inviting the three of them to sit at the table where I offer them the starter – mushroom tartlets, followed by a lamb tagine, both of which are greeted with appreciative murmurs. I've recently discovered that I find cooking therapeutic – something which would have amused Stella who I don't recall ever producing a proper meal. 'Why bother to cook?' she used to say. 'It's just a waste of time. You can always eat out or get a takeaway.'

I wonder whether Hugh and her previous partners shared that view.

The subject of homelessness is dropped while we eat, and we continue to converse in a more light-hearted vein.

'Come on, Hanna, show us the masterpieces you've been producing,' JC declares after the meal's over and the four of us are finishing the wine.

I take them into the tiny room (it's not grand enough to call a studio) where I do my painting, and show them the artwork I've nearly completed for the book about the girl and the elves.

JC studies the illustrations and remains silent for a moment before exclaiming sharply, 'But that's Stella!'

Maria and Sarah, neither of whom was well acquainted with Stella, regard him in surprise.

He frowns. 'Why have you painted Stella?'

I feel embarrassed just as I did when Aidan had a similar reaction. 'I didn't mean to. It just happened.'

'It seems a bit…spooky.'

I force a laugh. 'I know. I didn't intend to make the girl look like Stella. I'm sure a psychiatrist might have something to say about it. But once I'd done the first illustrations, the author and publisher liked them, so I had to keep the face the same throughout.'

JC peers closely at my later depictions of the girl. 'Her expressions are… kind of weird. She starts off looking angelic but then the face changes. She looks almost evil in that one.' He points at one of the final pictures I've produced.

I have to admit his observation is correct: the expression I've painted on the girl's face is verging on malicious.

Sarah appears to notice my discomfiture. 'Shut up, JC, I think they're brilliant,' she says sharply.

'So do I,' murmurs Maria.

'I didn't say the pictures weren't good,' JC assures me, looking a little flustered. 'It's just a bit…disturbing to see Stella's face, that's all, after --'

'Come on, JC.' Sarah gives his arm a shake. 'I think it's time we went home and relieved the babysitter.' She heads towards the door and, with an apologetic glance at me, JC follows.

After they've left, Maria and I have a final glass of wine together.

'Did you really not intend to draw Stella?' she asks.

'Absolutely. I was startled myself when I saw the resemblance. It's just one of those…odd things that happen, you know, after a person has died. But JC was right. It is a bit spooky.'

# Chapter 21

For several days I've been wondering whether to tell Aidan about my encounter with Damian Matthews and his story about the blackmail threat. He always looks troubled when Stella is mentioned and I wonder whether he needs to know that she wasn't the flawless creature he hungered after in the past. Will it harm if I don't tell him? After worrying about this for a while, I decide it's probably better if I do mention what Damian told me, especially as Aidan often asks if I know how the investigation's going.

We meet in a noisy pub and I wait until we manage to find a table where we can hear each other speak before mentioning the surprise visit from Damian.

'Damian Matthews?' Aidan's expression darkens and he slams his pint of beer down on the table, making me jump. 'That sleazebag Stella was with before Whitmore? Is he still around then?'

'He told me he moved to London some time ago but he's working back here at the moment, making a documentary about local building developments.'

'Oh?' Aidan's mouth twists contemptuously. 'I thought betting shops and casinos were more his line of business.'

I swallow hard. 'I'm afraid he told me something rather disturbing...about Stella.'

Aidan looks startled. 'What?'

He gazes at me in astonishment when I repeat what Damian told me about Regency Towers and Stella's threat to blackmail Hugh, then shakes his head emphatically.

'I don't believe that for a moment. It can't be true. I've no doubt Whitmore was responsible for the building fiasco, but Stella would never have been mixed up in anything like that.' He says this almost accusingly as if he thinks I've invented the story.

'I found it impossible to believe at first too,' I tell him. 'I thought the story was crazy. I know Hugh was an absolute bastard to Stella, but it's hard to credit that she would go so far as to blackmail him. On the other hand, I don't think Damian could have made it up; he was far too anxious to find out whether the police knew he was involved.'

Aidan's expression relaxes. 'In that case, the whole thing must have been his idea from the start. Stella may have had nothing to do with it.'

A loud gale of laughter from a nearby table prevents me from commenting and I wait until the noise dies down before replying.

'That also occurred to me but the detective told me the police have questioned both him and Hugh about the blackmail story, and Hugh said it was only Stella who tried to extort money from him. He didn't mention Damian at all; he didn't know Damian had anything to do with the idea, so I'm afraid Damian's in the clear.' I glance at Aidan wondering how he'll react.

He looks defeated and mutters, 'Well, I expect Stella just wanted Whitmore to get his comeuppance. And who can blame her?'

'Not me! But if it *is* true, why didn't Hugh just report

the blackmail threat to the police? I'm sure they would have acted. He was exonerated at the Regency Towers enquiry after all, and he's a prominent local businessman.'

Aidan gazes pensively into his pint of beer. 'Maybe he didn't report it precisely *because* he's a prominent local businessman. He had his professional reputation to consider. If his responsibility for the Regency Towers fiasco leaked out it might have jeopardised his business; *Whitmore Futures* could have gone down the tubes.' He frowns then his expression suddenly changes. 'What if it was *Matthews* who killed Stella?' he suggests eagerly. 'He could have been desperate to get his hands on the whole fifty grand to pay off his gambling debts.'

'That occurred to me as well, but the police say Hugh insists he never gave her the money. And Damian says he's been going home to Wimbledon every weekend since he started working on the documentary. I'm sure the police will have followed that up. They still think there's little doubt that Hugh's the one who killed her.'

I feel overwhelmed with sudden grief. Although the initial feelings of desolation provoked by Stella's death have receded and my nightmares have become less frequent, it still sometimes hits me with a force of a blow – usually when I'm least expecting it – that she's no longer here. Tears start pricking my eyelids. 'I wish I'd never heard about the rotten business, Aidan. It's bad enough that Stella's been murdered, but finding out that she was capable of blackmail on top of everything else… it's unbearable.'

Aidan takes my hand. 'I'm sorry, Hanna. She was your friend for so long, it must be hard to find out that she wasn't… she wasn't the person you thought…that *any* of us thought… she was.'

The kindness in his voice prompts the wretched tears to flow. I dab furiously at my eyes but to no avail. Aidan puts his arm around me and I lean my head against his shoulder and weep.

He waits for the tears to subside. 'Are you OK?' he asks when they finally do.

'Yes,' I snuffle. Straightening up, I blow my nose and try to compose myself. To my mortification I notice that the people sitting at nearby tables are watching us curiously. 'Sorry. This happens to me sometimes; it's a legacy of the head injury. I can't help it.'

Aidan gets up and goes to the bar. When he comes back he thrusts a small glass into my hand. 'Drink this; it's brandy. It'll make you feel better.'

He sits and watches me silently as I sip it and after I put the glass down, asks me again, 'Are you OK?'

'Yes.' The brandy has left a pleasurable burn inside my throat.

'Still getting the headaches?'

'Occasionally.'

'What about your memory? Has there been any improvement?'

'No. Maybe I'll never remember what happened that night.'

He pushes his fair hair back from his forehead. 'Well as you said yourself, that's probably for the best, isn't it? If you did remember, it could be too distressing.'

'Yes, you're probably right.' As I pick up the glass and take another sip, I hear him softly humming a tune to himself.

After I've finished the brandy, he stands up. Catching me by the hand, he pulls me to my feet. 'Come on. Let's go.'

'Where?'

He smiles. 'Back to my place.'

'Your place?' I'm surprised; I've never been asked to his house before.

'Yes, if you don't mind walking. I didn't bring the car because I knew I'd be drinking, but it's not far.'

He leads me out of the pub and we walk through the dark streets for about fifteen minutes before stopping at a terraced house in a road near Fiveways. He unlocks the front door and turns on a hall light. 'Welcome to my humble abode.'

I have the impression that the house is dark and rather empty. Aidan doesn't show me the ground floor. He takes me straight upstairs to a bedroom where, overcome with surprise and delight, I let him undress me. He lays me gently on a double bed as though I'm a sick child, then makes tender love to me.

\* \* \*

I wake to find I'm alone in a strange bed. It takes me a while to realise where I am and when I remember what happened the previous night and relive the memory of Aidan's lovemaking, I experience little shudders of excitement. After a few minutes, he enters the room. He's fully dressed and carrying a steaming mug which he places on the bedside table.

'Awake?' He smiles at me. 'I've made you some tea. I have to get off to work now.'

Remembering the intimacy of his caresses and the gentleness with which he entered me, I feel overwhelmed with sudden shyness.

He sits down on the bed and strokes my hair. 'Help yourself to breakfast in the kitchen – I've left cereal and bread out for you. There's coffee in the cupboard, milk and the usual stuff in the fridge. Just pull the front door shut on the Yale lock when you leave. I'll call you later.' He leans down and kisses me gently on the mouth, then rises to his feet and leaves the room.

After I hear him leave the house, I drink the tea then get up, put on a dressing gown that's hanging on the back of the door and go for a wander around the house. I peer nosily into every room. Although it must be at least a year since Aidan's divorce, they all seem rather bare and functional, as though he's only recently moved in. The large living room is sparsely furnished, containing just a sofa, a leather armchair, a coffee table, a sound system with large speakers, a cabinet full of CDs and a wide screen TV. There are no photographs or pictures on the walls and no ornaments on the bookshelves in the recesses on both sides of the fireplace. I wonder if his ex wife took all their more intimate possessions after the divorce.

The kitchen is also fairly spartan: it's neat and clean, but devoid of the usual utensils and pieces of culinary equipment one would expect to see on the worktops. I conclude from this that Aidan doesn't cook very often.

Feeling too excited to eat any breakfast, I go upstairs to the bathroom where I sniff Aidan's soap and aftershave. They have a familiar musky smell that I now associate with him. I sing to myself as I shower and dress.

When I leave the house the world appears freshly painted in wonderful bright colours. It's a clear sunny morning, the sky is a flawless blue and everything smells fresh and new. I'm in such a state of euphoria that I almost dance my way home.

I am a blackbird singing in the morning; I am a flower unfurling my petals after a long, hard winter; I am the sun emerging from behind purple-black clouds… I have never felt like this before. I'm *in love*!

I'm thirty nine, for God's sake, yet I feel as giddy as a schoolgirl.

# Chapter 22

Aidan and I now spend nights together several times a week, either at his house or, less frequently, in my flat (his bed is bigger and more comfortable for two than mine). We are "an item" – a couple – and I'm consumed with happiness.

In my euphoria I forget all about Robbie Cole until I return to Hove one day to pick up some art materials I've ordered, and spot him slumped against the window of the same shop where I encountered him the first time. His appearance is unkempt, his eyes are shut and he looks ill and drawn. Discarded sandwich wrappers and empty drink cans are strewn messily around his feet.

I stop in front of him. 'Robbie?'

He opens his eyes and blinks at me without recognition.

'It's Hanna. We had a chat recently, remember?'

He seems to recognise me now and gives a slight nod.

'Are you OK?'

'Yeah.' His voice is hoarse.

'You don't look OK. What's wrong?'

'Just tired --' His voice is lost in a fit of coughing.

I'm concerned. 'It sounds like more than tiredness to me. Can I get you something?'

'Water.' He starts coughing again and covers his mouth with his hand.

I wait until the paroxysm has subsided. 'Look, I'm just going to pick up some stuff from a shop then I'll bring you some water on my way back, OK?'

He doesn't answer and I continue to the art suppliers. After I've collected the items I ordered, I go to a supermarket and buy some fruit and a bottle of water. I take them to Robbie who's still slumped against the wall in front of the shop. He accepts them with a mutter of thanks.

While he's eating a banana, I gather up the litter around his feet and drop it in the nearest bin.

He looks embarrassed and mumbles, 'I was going to do that myself; didn't get round to it.' After gulping some water, he starts coughing again.

I hover uncertainly in front of him for a moment, reluctant to walk away leaving him in this condition. 'You're not fit enough to sleep outside,' I tell him, 'especially now that the nights are getting colder.'

He gives a wry laugh.' What do you suggest I do? Book a room in *The Grand*?'

'Isn't there anyone who can help you?'

He shrugs. 'You mean like Mother Theresa? Santa Claus?' He starts coughing again and takes another gulp of water from the bottle.

I arrive at a sudden decision. 'Why don't you come back with me, Robbie? There's a sofa-bed in my living room. You can stay with me till you manage to sort yourself out.'

His eyes widen. 'What?'

'I said you can come and stay at my place for a while. It's not very big but it'll be a lot better than sleeping here, on the pavement'

'*Your* place?' He blinks at me. 'What's the catch?'

'There's no catch. It's a genuine offer. I don't like seeing you like this. It'll just be till you feel better; find a job.'

He looks confused. 'I dunno. It wouldn't be right…I mean, you don't know me from Adam.'

'That's true, but I'll take the risk.' I realise that I'm being impetuous and probably reckless, but this seems right.

He stares at me with an expression that implies he doesn't believe me. After a moment he mutters, 'Thanks, it's a nice offer, but it wouldn't be fair. What'll your family say if you turn up with me?'

'Nothing, because it's just me. I live on my own.'

'No, I …' Before he can finish the sentence, he has another fit of coughing and wipes his nose and mouth with a piece of rag.

'Robbie, you're not well. You'll be far better off in the warm at my place.'

He shakes his head. 'No. You wouldn't want me under your feet. It could take me a long time to find another job.'

'That doesn't matter. You can't stay here in your condition. Are you coming or not?'

It takes me a long time to convince him that I'm serious, but eventually he agrees, too weak to hold out against my stronger will.

The two of us gather up his sleeping bag and grubby bundles of possessions, and coughing intermittently, he accompanies me to the nearest bus stop.

The other passengers stare at us when we board the bus, some with open hostility, probably because Robbie looks so scruffy (and to be honest, he doesn't smell too good either).

When we arrive at my flat, I cram his belongings into the small utility room by the front door, hand him my dressing gown and, with some difficulty, persuade him to undress and give me his clothes. While he's having a shower, I put them in the washing machine and prepare him a quick meal of eggs on toast. He gobbles it down so voraciously that I realise he can't have eaten properly for some time. When his plate is empty, I make him a hot drink and give him a couple of Paracetamol tablets. I open up the sofa-bed on which, although it's still only early afternoon, he lies down and falls instantly asleep. He stays asleep for the rest of the day, and then all night.

He sleeps during much of the next day as well. When he finally gets up in the evening, he looks a lot better and his cough is less pronounced. I find him a razor and return his washed and ironed clothes. Clean-shaven and dressed, he looks like a different person.

I make us both a meal and while we're eating, he tells me more about his circumstances.

'My mother remarried and I didn't get on with my new stepfather, so I left home in Manchester and moved to London where I managed to get a job in an electronics company. After I met Alison, we decided to move to Brighton together. We thought the quality of life would be better here, ha ha! I got a new job and Ali got one as a receptionist and by a stroke of good luck – or so we believed – we managed to rent one of the small flats on the ground floor of the new Regency Towers block. We lived there for over a year until that day when everyone was evacuated. There were about sixty occupants altogether, I think, and we were all put up in hotels and B and Bs. We thought it would just be temporary but, like I told you before, Ali and me got stuck forever in a basement room. No-one cared about what happened to us next. At least that's how it seemed.'

I utter a murmur of sympathy.

'There was one guy, the one who bought the penthouse at the top – Cottram his name was --.'

'*Steve* Cottram?' I remember the detective telling me that he'd bought the penthouse.

Robbie looks surprised. 'You know him?'

'I used to know him. What about him?'

'He tried to get a bunch of us who'd lived in the Towers to join some kind of protest action. He said we needed to push for collective compensation, but after I left the B and B, I lost touch with what was going on.'

'Did the protest achieve anything?' The Steve Cottram I remember wouldn't have done anything that wasn't in his own self-interest.

Robbie shrugs. 'Dunno. I haven't seen any of the other residents since. Anyway, that's enough of my story.'

Feeling I should reciprocate with some information about myself, I give him a resumé of my life to date, concluding with an abbreviated account of what happened on the night of Stella's party.

He drops his fork and gazes at me, appalled. 'Come again? You're telling me that someone killed your best friend then attacked you?'

'Yes that's exactly what happened. Her ex husband's in custody. He's been charged with murder.' (I don't reveal that the person charged is the same person who was responsible for the collapse of Regency Towers, as DI Forrester has advised me to be circumspect in what I say to people). 'I've been suffering from Traumatic Brain Injury, and I can't remember anything about that night. I've been told I may never remember what happened.'

Robbie's expression has become troubled. 'Bloody hell, Hanna, that's ... terrible. I feel awful. I've been telling you my sob story when yours is so much worse than mine.' He reaches across the table and takes my hand. 'You're a very decent person, taking me into your home after what happened to you.'

'*Both* of us have been through a lot,' I mumble and to hide my embarrassment, jump up on pretence of fetching a glass of water.

# Chapter 23

My flat is very small and it's not ideal having someone sleeping in the living room, but Robbie is so grateful that he tries to keep out of my way as much as possible. A few days after moving in with me, he goes to sign on at the Job Centre. While he's out, Maria calls by with my mail which she's picked up in the communal postbox downstairs. I introduced Robbie to her shortly after bringing him home with me, and although she was ostensibly sympathetic to his plight, it was clear from her shocked expression that she disapproved of my letting him stay in my flat.

'Are you sure you're doing the right thing, Hanna?' she asks on discovering I'm alone. 'After all you've been through, you should be looking after *yourself*, not taking care of some waif and stray you've literally plucked off the streets.'

'I couldn't leave Robbie on the streets, Maria. He was too unwell.'

'I accept that he's fallen on hard times, but how much do you actually know about him?'

'Enough to know he's a decent man, Maria.'

She looks dubious. 'If you say so. But you know it's against your tenancy agreement to have a lodger. You could lose the flat.'

'Robbie's not a lodger. He's just a …friend who's staying with me for a while until he sorts himself out.'

'A friend?' Maria shakes her head. 'How long have you known him?'

'Only a few weeks; well, actually only a couple of days, but enough to--'

'A couple of days?' She looks appalled. 'How long do you think he'll be staying with you?'

'Just until he gets on his feet again, and finds a job.'

'And how long will that take?' She flaps her hands at me in a gesture of despair. 'I hope you know what you're doing, Hanna. It seems extremely risky to me. And what does Aidan think?' (She knows about my relationship with Aidan and does approve of that).

'I'm not seeing him till the weekend so I haven't mentioned it to him yet, but I'm sure he'll be OK with it,' I say without conviction.

* * *

Although I've been expecting Aidan to express similar reservations to Maria's, I'm taken aback by the ferocity of his reaction. When we meet for lunch in a restaurant on Saturday and I inform him that Robbie is staying in my living room, he goes silent for a moment then his face reddens. 'Staying in *your flat*? A *rough sleeper*? Are you mad, Hanna?'

'It seemed the right thing to do,' I mutter defensively.

'The *right* thing? What in God's name possessed you to put up a complete stranger? What do you know about him? He could be a criminal or a druggie.'

'He isn't either,' I protest.

'How do you know he isn't? How long have you known him?'

'I only met Robbie in the last few weeks, but I know he's perfectly OK.'

'That's nonsense.' Aidan pushes his floppy hair away from his forehead in an angry gesture. 'Nobody can tell what a person's like after such a short time. You're putting yourself at risk, Hanna. You've already been attacked once, haven't you? You've got to get rid of him and the sooner the better. Tell him to go.'

'I can't do that, Aidan, he hasn't been well, and Robbie would never attack anyone.'

But Aidan's not mollified. 'I expect he gave you an elaborate sob story, didn't he? You're a soft touch, Hanna, far too generous for your own good. But listen to me; you can't let this guy take advantage of your kind heart and sponge off you indefinitely.'

'Robbie's *not* sponging off me,' I splutter indignantly. 'He came at my suggestion. He was ill and I insisted.' This is the first argument I've had with Aidan and I feel the tears welling up. 'Look, Hugh Whitmore's responsible for a lot of people becoming homeless, and if I can help one of them, it's the least I can do. Can't we talk about something else?'

Aidan grunts with irritation and slaps his knife down with a clang on the table. He doesn't say any more for a while and starts humming a low tune, as he often does when he's thinking or feeling emotional, but this time it's an urgent, rather unpleasant sound. He insists on coming home with me after lunch to vet Robbie whom he interrogates in a brusque, almost aggressive fashion.

Robbie responds to his questions in a dignified, restrained way and I can tell that Aidan's impressed in spite of himself. I'm both startled and thrilled by the vehemence of his reaction which I realise is prompted by concern for me tinged (I hope) with jealousy, for now that Robbie's clean-shaven and dressed in fresh clothes, it's obvious that he's a very good-looking young man. He's also polite and well-spoken and displays no sign of being either a criminal or a "druggie".

When I apologise to him later for Aidan's sharpness, he shrugs it off.

'It's understandable. He's your guy; of course he's worried about you. If I was in his shoes I'd be suspicious of me too!'

Unfortunately my new living situation creates a hiccup in my developing relationship with Aidan. Having someone sleeping in such close proximity to my bedroom means that it's preferable to make love at his place. But Aidan's continuing suspicion of Robbie and his fear that he might ransack my flat if I'm away from home overnight, somewhat dampens his ardour, and this temporarily obliges us to stop spending nights together. I find this extremely difficult for by now I'm totally addicted to Aidan – his voice, his touch, his smell. He's become like a drug I can't do without. Even so, I feel I can't tell Robbie to go. And far from ransacking the flat, he makes a point of tidying and cleaning it.

'You don't have to do that,' I tell him.

'It's the least I can do until I can pay my way,' he responds with a shy smile. 'I'm used to living in a small space and keeping it tidy after spending over a year in that crummy B and B. I promise I'll be out of your hair as soon as I get a job.'

Now that he's feeling so much better, he goes to the nearest library during the day and uses the computers provided there in his search for a job. In the evenings, he's touchingly worried about sharing my meals without contributing to the cost of them, although I assure him it isn't a problem. In fact I enjoy having the company. If he happens to be in the flat while I'm working during the day, he brings me cups of tea and coffee. He's fascinated by my artwork and asks intelligent questions about how I set about doing illustrations. A skilful handyman, he mends several of my appliances that haven't been working properly. Maria is totally won over when he repairs some faulty light switches in her flat.

Whereas most of my acquaintances are horrified at my rashness, as they see it, of allowing a stranger – and even worse, a homeless man – to sleep in my living room, JC, bless him, reacts very differently. He not only applauds my action, he also takes Robbie under his wing and attempts to help him get back on his feet. After only a couple of weeks, he manages to find him a temporary job as an electrician in the firm where he's engaged in upgrading the computers.

Robbie is over the moon and not long afterwards, he informs me that one of the other workers at the company has offered him a room in his house for a nominal rent. I'm rather sorry to see him go. I've become fond of him and will miss his quiet and unassuming presence. But it's a relief to have the flat back to myself, and of course I'm delighted to be able to resume my night-time trysts with Aidan.

Aidan declares himself greatly relieved. 'You got off very lightly…' he informs me, '…considering how foolhardy you were to put up someone you barely knew; a rough sleeper.'

I remain silent as I don't want to argue with him.

'But the best thing …' he adds, pulling me to him '…is that now I can have you all to myself again.'

# Chapter 24

Despite the traumatic and life-changing attack I suffered on the night of Stella's party, I'm actually feeling happier and more secure than I've felt for a long time. Professionally things have been going really well and I've received several new commissions to illustrate children's books. The one about the girl and the elves has received excellent reviews and one critic has even made a point of mentioning how my illustrations have "cleverly hinted at a certain darkness in the heroine's otherwise seemingly innocent character".

My personal life has also improved greatly since Aidan and I resumed our interrupted love affair. We see each other frequently, go on regular outings together, and occasionally meet for meals with JC and Sarah, although the imminent birth of their third child has begun to curtail their social activities. After the brief hiatus in our relationship, Aidan seems to want to spend as much time with me as possible before a big job he has lined up in Tunbridge Wells. He has even suggested that we spend a weekend together somewhere. The prospect of having several days alone with him gives me pleasurable prickles of excitement.

We leave on a Friday and drive to a delightful place on the Suffolk coast. We stay in a charming B and B and make love each night in a large and rather lumpy double bed. The autumn weather is fine and bracing and we spend the days taking long walks. The sea air is very different to that in Brighton, and I find it relaxing. We take the ferry across the River Blyth to Southwold; enjoy meals at lovely old pubs and visit Aldeburgh where we browse the High Street and sample fish and chips on the seafront. I enjoy it all and am in seventh heaven, except for one thing...

Something has happened. I don't want to make too much of it, but it has upset me. Normally Aidan is a very gentle lover, but for some reason, last night at the B and B, he was much rougher; more passionate. I didn't mind that – in fact I rather liked it! But here's the thing: when he climaxed, he shouted '*Stella!*' in a very emotional way. He apologised afterwards, of course; said he didn't know why it had happened. But that hasn't stopped me feeling upset and wondering whether, in some weird way, I'm acting as a proxy for Stella when we make love. I look nothing like her (unfortunately) and our personalities are very different, but maybe because of my long connection with her, Aidan does consider me as a kind of surrogate.

It's not pleasant to feel that the person making love to you is actually thinking of someone else, and this has somewhat depressed my spirits. However, I'm reluctant to question Aidan too closely on the nature of his feelings for me in case I don't like how he responds. I know he likes me and ostensibly enjoys being with me, but he's never said that he loves me. Perhaps, after being abandoned by his wife and what happened to Stella, he just needed a woman in his life and I happened to come along at the right time. Or is that selling myself too short? Anyway, I suspect his feelings towards me are confused, so I've decided I must try not to dwell on this and enjoy the rest of our short break together.

# Chapter 25

Aidan has started working in Tunbridge Wells. This means he has to leave early in the morning during the week and doesn't get home till fairly late in the evening. By then he's usually too tired to do anything other than have a light supper and go to bed. I've tried, not entirely successfully, to erase what happened during our weekend in Suffolk from my mind, and he's been very attentive towards me ever since. He calls me every day to ask how I am, and leaves affectionate messages on my phone when he can't get hold of me. As it's difficult to get together during the week, we arrange to meet on Saturday evening. I can't see him earlier that day as I've received an invitation from Stella's parents to visit them for tea.

* * *

It's with some trepidation that I take the train to Hassocks. Although I'm fond of the old couple, I anticipate some heart-wrenching reminiscences about the past and the youthful experiences Stella and I shared.

Mr Knight meets me at the station and drives me to their cottage, a quintessentially English one with a large, well-tended garden and a lovely view of the South Downs. As he parks the car, the front door opens and a little white dog scampers out, followed by Mrs Knight. My heart sinks when I notice how slowly and stiffly she now walks. It's the first time I've seen them since they visited me in hospital and once again I'm struck by how old and frail they both look. Stella's death seems to have aged them by about ten years.

Mrs Knight's lower lip quivers as soon as she sees me. Taking my hands in hers, she grips them tightly. 'It's so good to see you, Hanna.'

'Thank you for inviting me.'

'Are you quite better now, dear?' she asks, scrutinising my face. 'It was a terrible thing that happened to you.'

'Yes, thank you, Mrs Knight. I feel much better.'

'That's good.' She looks me up and down and tuts. 'You've lost such a lot of weight, but you look really well. Doesn't she look well, Roger? Blooming.'

'She does, she does,' her husband agrees, 'blooming.'

I thank them but can't help feeling guilty for looking "blooming" when all that's left of their daughter are her ashes in Brighton Cemetery.

'Quiet, Harvey!' Mr Knight bends and fondles the dog that's yapping and worrying around our legs, trying to get our attention.

'How are the headaches now, dear?' Mrs Knight asks, continuing to grip my hands.

'Not quite so bad, thank you.'

'And what about your memory; has it returned yet?'

'No, I'm afraid I still can't remember what happened on the night of the party.'

'That's probably just as well.' She relinquishes my hands. 'But at least we know who did it now.' Her expression hardens. 'Thank God the police have caught that monster,

Hugh Whitmore. I wish Stella had never set eyes on him. I always said it wouldn't work out, didn't I, Roger? The man's a devil. I wish we still had the death penalty in this country.'

'Steady on, Margaret,' her husband mumbles. 'He'll get Life, we can be sure of that.'

'He didn't allow Stella to keep *her* life,' she counters fiercely, 'so why should he keep *his*? True justice should be a life for a life.'

Mr Knight puts a gentle hand on her shoulder. 'Well, don't let's dwell on that now. Can't we just enjoy Hanna's visit?'

Her lip quivers again so I quickly interject, 'I went to see Stella's plaque in the Garden of Remembrance. Those red roses are gorgeous, Mrs Knight.'

She looks surprised. '*Red* roses? No, dear. We arranged to have a pre-planted rose bush by the plaque, but I specified *white* roses. You remember how much Stella loved roses?'

'Yes of course.' I'm puzzled. 'There was a beautiful bouquet of red roses lying in front of her plaque. The card said she would always be loved. It wasn't from you?'

'No, it wasn't from us. It must have been from one of her friends.' She sighs. 'Stella had lots of friends, didn't she? And we were told we couldn't leave flowers by the memorial plaques; they had to be put somewhere else. But never mind that. Let's go inside now, it's getting chilly. The tea's all ready.'

She ushers me into the house and into a comfortably-furnished small room where an enormous spread of sandwiches, homemade scones and cakes has been laid out on the table. I gaze at it in consternation, fearing I'll be unable to do sufficient justice to such a feast. The little dog runs over to his basket in a corner and lies down in it.

As I'd feared, the conversation centres on Stella and before we have tea, Mrs Knight produces a bulky album of photographs of her taken from when she was a small child. She invites me to sit between her and her husband on the sofa to look through it. Unsurprisingly the pictures confirm that Stella was an incredibly beautiful little girl and tears flow freely down the old couple's cheeks as each page is turned.

When I remark on the absence of baby pictures, Mrs Knight turns to me with an expression of surprise. 'Of course I don't have any of those, dear. Stella was three when we got her.'

I'm astounded. '*Got* her? You mean she was--?'

'Yes, Stella was adopted, didn't you know?'

I feel a sense of shock. 'No, she never mentioned it. Nobody else did either.'

Mr Knight gives an embarrassed cough. 'Actually that was quite deliberate. After what she'd been through, we decided not to talk about the adoption, at least not while she was still so young. It didn't seem the right thing to do.'

*What does he mean, "What she'd been through"?*

'We didn't discuss it with her until she reached sixteen,' he continues, 'and we only did then because we thought she was old enough for us to broach the subject. As you know, people have a right to contact their birthparents these days. But Stella was furious when we brought the subject up, wasn't she, Margaret?'

Yes, very angry.' Mrs Knight seems about to cry again and I notice that her hand holding the photo album, has started to tremble. 'She shouted at us... almost accused us of inventing the story; she said we were lying!'

'Why would she do that?' I ask, intrigued.

The old man's expression becomes troubled. 'We wondered whether it was because she could still remember something… unpleasant from her past, and didn't want to be reminded of it.'

'What could she have remembered?' I can't help asking.

Mr Knight glances quickly at his wife then at me. 'Well, I suppose there's no reason not to tell you. Social Services removed her from her parents because they found out she was being badly mistreated…by her father --'

'If he *was* her father,' Mrs Knight's face has turned mottled red with anger. 'Her mother had a reputation for sleeping around. The man was violent to the baby – to a *baby* would you believe – but that woman turned a blind eye. What a way to treat an innocent child! Someone alerted Social Services and when they went round they discovered she'd been brutalised and totally neglected.' Her eyes fill with tears again. 'Apparently there were bruises all over her body, poor little thing; even some broken bones.'

I gasp.

'Yes,' she continues. 'It was shocking. The case was in the papers. He got a couple of years for child cruelty and the mother got a suspended sentence for neglect; not nearly enough if you ask me. They should have been put away for years. Stella was taken into Care, then when she was well enough, put up for adoption. As we didn't have any children ourselves and seemed unlikely to as I was over forty, we applied, and eventually we managed to adopt her. The mother's parents contested it but they failed, thank God. We couldn't believe our luck. She was such a beautiful child. They called her Lorraine. We didn't like the name, so we called her Stella…our little star; our little angel.' The old woman's face becomes distorted with grief and her eyes brim with tears.

Mr Knight puts an arm around her and I notice that his own eyes are moist. 'Don't distress yourself, Margaret. We made up for what happened to her, didn't we? We did all we could. We gave her a good home during all those years. She had a very happy childhood in the end.' He takes the photo album from his wife and shuts it firmly. 'That's enough for now. Hanna's very kindly come to see us so let's have a nice tea and talk about something else.'

'Yes, of course; you're right.' Mrs Knight wipes her eyes and hauls herself to her feet with an effortful grunt. 'Come and have tea, Hanna. The kettle's already boiled.'

Mr Knight and I rise from the sofa and sit at the table while she bustles around us pouring tea and offering us plates piled with sandwiches, cakes and scones. I eat as much as I can manage while trying to sustain a rather stilted conversation. In between exhorting me to accept more of the food (for, in Mrs Knight's opinion, I've lost far too much weight), the old couple ask me polite questions about my flat, my work and mutual acquaintances. I answer mechanically as my mind is elsewhere, buzzing with the information I've just received. In all those years I was friends with Stella, she never once breathed a word about being adopted. It did occasionally strike me that she bore no resemblance to either of her parents, but I always assumed she'd inherited her extraordinary looks from some earlier ancestor. Could she have been ashamed of being adopted? Maybe it was something she liked to think hadn't happened or, more likely, that she wanted to forget. How much *do* toddlers retain of traumatic early experiences? If Stella was already three when she was removed from her birth parents, she might not have completely forgotten the occasions when her father (if he *was* her father) acted violently towards her. Such memories must have left an indelible mark on her psyche. Poor Stella. I feel a hot rush of sympathy for what she must have suffered as a tiny child and cold fury towards the callous perpetrator and his unfeeling wife. I wonder how *I* would have reacted if I'd been adopted and reminded of my horrendous early circumstances when I reached my teens. Maybe Mr and Mrs Knight should have waited until Stella was a bit older before bringing the subject up, although I'm sure they thought they were doing the right thing.

I'm immersed in these thoughts when Mrs Knight asks me suddenly, 'Would you be kind enough to do something for us, dear?'

'Of course. What is it?'

'Stella's flat has been re-let and it has to be emptied next week. Roger's arranged for all the furniture and kitchen stuff to be collected for auction. But there's still her clothes and all her personal belongings to pack up…' Her face crumples. 'And I can't bring myself to--'

'Would you like me to do it?'

Although the thought of returning to the flat is just as horrifying for me, I can understand the woman's reluctance to sort through her daughter's clothes and personal effects; the renewed grief it must arouse.

The relief on Mrs Knight's face is adequate reward for my courage. 'Would you, dear? I'd be so grateful. And of course, if there are any of her things you'd like to keep, please feel free to take them. Otherwise…maybe charity shops?'

'Don't worry,' I assure her, 'I'll think of somewhere to take them. But surely you don't want it all to be given away or sold. Wouldn't you like to keep some of her things? What about valuable stuff, like jewellery and ornaments?'

She looks confused. 'I don't know. I'll leave you to decide, dear. If there's anything you think we should keep, maybe put it aside and give it to us another time. It's just for now I can't face-- '

'I understand. When would you like me to do it?'

'The furniture's being removed next Thursday and the flat has to be completely emptied by the end of the week,' Mr Knight tells me. 'So any day that suits you before then, if it's not too inconvenient. I'll give you a spare key and if you wouldn't mind putting it through the letterbox when you've finished,' He takes a key from a desk drawer and hands it to me. 'Thank you, Hanna. We really appreciate it.'

As it's getting late, I decide it's time to leave. I thank them profusely and promise I'll visit them again soon.

Mrs Knight accompanies me to the door and presses a bag of apples from the garden and a tin containing some of her homemade scones, into my hands. She sheds a few more tears as she says goodbye. 'Do come back and visit us again, dear. It can get a bit lonely here with just me, Roger and Harvey.'

I assure her I will.

Mr Knight drives me back to the station and hugs me when we part. 'Margaret will never get over this, Hanna,' he tells me unnecessarily. 'Neither will I, of course. But what can we do? Stella's gone and that's all there is to it. We can't get her back so we just have to accept it.' His face is a mask of tragedy.

The tears I've been holding back with difficulty all afternoon start trickling down my face.

* * *

The revelations about Stella's early years and the discovery that she was adopted, force me to view her in a different and more understanding light. I've read enough to know that our earliest years are crucial to our future development, and I'm aware that the care and emotional support we receive during those years can have a critical impact on our personalities, as well as on all our social and personal relationships. I'm not an expert in psychology, but I can't help wondering whether Stella had subconsciously accepted that male abuse was her lot in life.

The resentment I've been feeling because she kept so much from me melts away, and I'm filled with guilt for harbouring such ambivalent thoughts about her. I resolve that from now on I will dwell only on the happy memories of our long friendship.

When I meet Aidan in the evening I describe my visit to Stella's parents. He's as astonished as I was to learn that she was adopted. 'I never knew that. She never mentioned it to you?'

'No, she never told me or anyone else as far as I know. I think it was something she wanted to forget. Apparently her birth parents were appalling – violent and neglectful.'

I repeat the details of Stella's early life that Mr and Mrs Knight related to me.

As I speak, his expression becomes agonised. 'I wish I'd known. Poor Stella. '

# Chapter 26

It's my second visit to Stella's flat since she died and I find it just as harrowing as the first. In fact I can't stop trembling with nervousness when I unlock the front door and let myself in. Avoiding the kitchen, I head directly to the bedroom where there are two built-in wardrobes, both full to bursting with expensive designer clothes. I remember Stella wearing a number of them on specific occasions, always looking extremely elegant. I remove all the garments, fold them, and stuff them into bin bags which I leave in the hall ready to take to local charity shops when Maria comes to collect me. She has kindly offered to drive me to them in her car.

I empty the drawers containing Stella's nightclothes and underwear, then the closet containing her jackets, coats and jumpers, and fill six more bags with them. I don't keep any of the garments for myself. Lovely as they are, there's no way I could bear to wear any of Stella's things (despite the fact that, amazingly, they would probably fit me now.)

I pack yet more black bags with her shoes and boots. She had an astonishing number of them, many of them brand new and still wrapped in tissue paper in boxes bearing the names of famous footwear designers. 'Whenever are you ever going to wear all these shoes?' I once asked Stella when she showed me the boxes piled high in her hall cupboard.

She gave her familiar tinkling laugh. 'You don't have to wear them all. Just *having* them is what matters.'

I couldn't understand this view and concluded it must be extremely prosaic of me to believe that shoes were just for wearing on ones feet.

The dressing table drawers contain cases of Stella's jewellery, many pieces of which I recognise – eye-wateringly expensive gifts from her succession of men friends which she always showed me proudly after they were presented to her. I place the jewellery in a box which I'll take home with me and keep for Mr and Mrs Knight.

Next I gather up the framed photographs displayed around the living room. Sadly there aren't any among them picturing Stella with her parents. I pack the majority of the photos in a bag that I'll give to the old couple. Despite their understandable reluctance to handle their daughter's effects, I believe they might want to keep these as mementoes when the initial searing pain of her death begins to fade.

I decide to keep some of the photos myself, the handful of Stella and me together in former years, despite the sadness I know I'll experience whenever I look at them.

The pile of birthday gifts – some still in their colourful wrapping paper – presents me with a dilemma, so I leave it till last. Should these brand new and expensive items be returned to the donors, or should I add them to the bags destined for charity shops? I conclude that this isn't my problem: it will be up to Stella's parents to decide what to do with them. I fill two more bags with the gifts and add them to the ones I'll take home with me. (I gave Stella my own birthday present – a portrait I painted of her in secret – before the party. She was delighted with it and hung it on the living room wall. That too will go to her parents).

I have to force myself to enter the kitchen. I drag the boxes of empty bottles and bag of discarded beer cans through to the living room then into the hall and add them to the pile destined for recycling. There are now so many bags lined up by the front door that it's obvious that they won't all fit into Maria's small car. I ring and warn her we may need to make several trips.

Finally I visit the bathroom and empty the cupboards containing Stella's extensive range of makeup and toiletries. I put the unopened packs and jars in a bag for the charity shops and the used stuff into one destined for the recycling centre. Seeing that Stella's bathrobe is still hanging on a hook on the back of the door, I take it down and slip my hand into the pockets to make sure there's nothing in them before I add the robe to one of the bags of clothes in the hall. In a small inner pocket I find a used tissue and a small, crumpled piece of paper. Some instinct prompts me to smooth out the paper and when I do, I reel with shock. It contains a single line of upper-case letters that have been cut out of a newspaper or magazine and pasted on. The words the letters compose read:

STELLA YOURE GOING TO GET WHATS COMING TO YOU BITCH

I'm so shaken that I have to sit down for a moment. Who could have sent Stella such a vile message? I can't believe it was Hugh. I can't imagine him painstakingly cutting letters out of a newspaper. If he wanted to threaten her, he would have used his phone or another sophisticated piece of modern technology rather than this crude method of communication. But if it wasn't Hugh, who was it? Did Stella have enemies I wasn't aware of? How devastated she must have been if she went into the hall after a leisurely bath and discovered this on her doormat.

I ring DI Forrester and tell him what I've found. He says he'll call on me later and examine the note. I wonder if it will have any bearing on the murder enquiry. In the meantime I show it to Maria when she comes to collect the bags of Stella's belongings.

'Wow!' she exclaims, 'that's horrendous. Do you think her ex husband sent it?'

'No, he was certainly capable of threatening her, but I doubt he would have done it this way. In fact I can't think of anyone these days who would go to the trouble of sending this kind of anonymous message.'

The detective arrives several hours after we've returned from delivering Stella's belongings to several charity shops and the recycling centre. There were so many bags that, as expected, we had to make a number of journeys. Those I've kept for Stella's parents are crammed against the wall in my tiny hall.

DI Forrester looks puzzled when I show him the crumpled piece of paper.

'Well, well,' he muses, 'Stella certainly seems to have raised a few hackles one way or another.'

'Do you think it's connected with what happened to her?'

He frowns. 'Maybe.'

I find this a deeply troubling possibility. 'But why would anyone contact her this way?' I ask. 'It's so crude.'

He scratches his head and studies the message again. 'Perhaps they thought it would be less... traceable than if they'd used a more sophisticated method of communication.'

'Is this kind of message untraceable?' I ask. 'I can't see how it would be possible to detect who sent it.'

'It won't be easy, but I'll see what my colleagues can do.'

'You don't think Hugh Whitmore could have sent it?'

He gives me a quizzical look. 'What do you think?'

'I think it's extremely unlikely. It's not Hugh's style. In fact I'd be amazed if he sent it, unless he was being devilishly clever and hoping a message like that would scare Stella into thinking someone else was after her.'

The detective looks dubious. 'That also seems extremely unlikely.'

He asks me not to mention the threatening message to anyone while it's being investigated. I don't admit that I've already shown it to Maria. And of course I don't mention it when I ring Stella's parents to tell them that I've taken Stella's clothes to charity shops but have kept a number of photographs, valuables and birthday presents for them to collect from me when they're ready.

Mr Knight says he'll call round for them after Stella's furniture has been removed.

# Chapter 27

I haven't heard back from DI Forrester so assume that the sender of the anonymous threat hasn't been traced. Although the discovery of the message has disturbed me profoundly, I'm trying not to dwell on it and am immersing myself in a newly commissioned piece of work – illustrating a futuristic book about children arriving on a new planet with their parents and meeting the resident aliens. The considerable demands the story makes on my imagination concentrate my mind to the exclusion of worrying thoughts.

\* \* \*

Robbie has kept in touch since he moved out of my flat and I'm pleased to hear that his job is going well. One evening he calls me in a state of euphoria. His employers have told him that, subject to a satisfactory review after he's worked there for six weeks, they're prepared to offer him a permanent contract. He thanks me effusively for this unanticipated piece of good luck. When I remind him that it was JC who found him the job, he insists that the upturn in his circumstances is entirely due to me for taking him into my home when he was at his lowest ebb. To express his gratitude, he says he would like to take me out for a meal one evening and brushes aside my protest that he should put his earnings towards finding new accommodation. I accept the invitation, but persuade him to choose an inexpensive restaurant: a small, recently-opened one that specialises in vegetarian food. Maria and I have eaten there once and were impressed. The dinner was excellent and the East European staff – defiantly still in the country despite the uncertainty concerning their future residential status – were polite and efficient.

Because of Aidan's hostile reaction to Robbie, I choose not to mention the arrangement to him as I don't want to spoil the renewed harmony in our relationship. Besides, I reason, I'm free to socialise with whoever I please, and it's not as if Robbie and I are anything more than friends, is it? (To tell the truth, it's a novel experience for me to have a lover who's jealous of my other male relationships, and I'm rather enjoying it!)

When I arrive at the restaurant, I find it's about three quarters full with a predominantly youthful clientele, many of them, I guess from their appearance, students.

Robbie is already sitting at a table and I'm delighted to see how well he's looking. He's put on weight; his crinkly black hair is neatly cut and he's wearing a crisp blue shirt and skinny jeans. I notice with amusement the admiring glances he's attracting from many of the young women in the restaurant. Not for the first time I wonder how, in this day and age, such a pleasant and personable young man could have been reduced to sleeping on the streets.

While we're eating, Robbie enthusiastically describes his new job, his colleagues and the room he's currently renting from one of them for a peppercorn rent. He's in high spirits. 'I'm hoping to save enough to get a flat soon,' he tells me.

'I've already started contacting estate agents. That reminds me: I bumped into that guy I told you about; the one who had the luxury penthouse in Regency Towers, Steve Cottram. He's still furious about what happened.'

'Is he?' I mutter without great interest.

'He says he's suing the developer as he's lost so much money.'

'Yes, so I heard.' I wonder how Hugh will continue to manage his business affairs while he's in prison but decide I don't care. As I don't want to think about Hugh Whitmore, I change the subject. 'This Jerusalem artichoke soup is delicious, isn't it?'

'Yes it is,' Robbie agrees. 'Cottram asked after you, Hanna.'

'Why on earth would Steve Cottram be interested in me?'

He seems surprised at the sharpness of my reaction. 'Probably because I mentioned you to him. You said you knew him.'

'Yes, so I did.' I remember that I haven't told Robbie about the relationship between Stella and Steve and the mutual dislike Steve and I had for each other.

'He said he'd like to see you again,' Robbie adds.

I almost drop my soup spoon. 'Why would he want to see *me* again?' I summon a casual laugh. 'I hope you didn't give him my number.'

Robbie looks embarrassed. 'No I didn't give him your number, but he wanted to know your address so I gave it to him.'

I can't prevent a grunt of annoyance. 'You what?'

He stares at me. 'Why? Is there a problem?'

I don't answer immediately. The prospect of coming face

to face with another of Stella's ghastly former lovers is deeply unpleasant, so I hope Steve's alleged desire to see me again was just one of those throwaway comments people tend to make during small talk.

Noticing Robbie's worried expression, I hasten to reassure him. 'No, it's not a problem. It's just that Steve Cottram and I weren't exactly…buddies. He was involved with my friend Stella. They lived together for a time.'

Robbie looks even more worried. 'Oh, you mean *that* friend; the one who …was killed.'

'Yes. Their relationship ended badly and Steve thought I'd influenced her; he believed I'd persuaded her to leave him, so as you can imagine, I wasn't his favourite person.'

'Oh, I see. I'm sorry; I didn't mean to…I mean I hope I haven't --'

'It's OK, Robbie; you weren't to know and it was a long time ago. Let's not talk about it.' I quickly steer the conversation into calmer waters.

After we leave the restaurant, Robbie walks me home and before we separate, he agrees to join Maria and me on one of our fortnightly meals out – my treat this time. I know Maria will be pleased as she now takes an almost maternal interest in Robbie. I don't blame her for her earlier suspicion of him as I know it was prompted by protectiveness towards me,

When I'm back in my flat, however, I find it difficult to sleep. The conversation with Robbie has aroused unpleasant memories of Steve Cottram that I can't shake off, and as I scroll mentally through my recollections of the doomed relationship between him and Stella, something suddenly occurs to me with the force of a hammer blow. That shadowy figure caught on CCTV late on the night of the party; the one emerging from the lower end of Stella's road who looked vaguely familiar... I now realise belatedly that it was *Steve Cottram*!

I haven't seen Steve for almost a decade. He would be in his mid forties by now and the chances are he will have changed a bit physically. But that walk! Steve had a jaunty, almost swaggering stride that the CCTV image managed to capture. When DI Forrester showed it to me, I was too tired and traumatised to think clearly and since then I'd forgotten all about it. Should I contact the detective and tell him what I've just remembered? His visits have become less frequent since Hugh was charged with Stella's murder, so the investigation may have been closed, in which case, will the information still be relevant? After restlessly weighing up the pros and cons, I conclude that I should tell him. After all, I did promise to call him as soon as I remembered anything – "anything at all".

But what would Steve have been doing in Stella's road at that time of night? Was he on his way to see her? If so, why? The detective told me he'd already contacted Stella to find out what she knew about Regency Towers, so why would he have needed to visit her again at such a late hour? I try to curb the lurid flights my imagination starts taking and to think rationally. Maybe Steve wasn't heading for Stella's flat at all; he could have been going anywhere. He might even have moved into that area.

As sleep continues to elude me, I reflect on the coincidence that three of Stella's former long-term partners have re-emerged in connection with her since she died. It strikes me that in each case the link is Regency Towers. Hugh was responsible for the building's conception and construction as well as for its collapse; Damian was seeking to capitalise on his discovery that it was Hugh's negligence that led to the building's disintegration, and Steve, who bought the penthouse in the Towers, is now is seeking compensation for its loss and the money he invested in it. Both Damian and Steve had something to gain from the knowledge that Hugh was responsible for the flaws in the building's structure. Both assumed that Stella would be privy to information about his role in the catastrophe and hoped that, after a bitter divorce, she might be ready and perhaps eager to disclose what she knew.

I wonder whether Steve is aware of the documentary Damian is making and whether there has been any communication between the two of them. It's an intriguing thought. They would have no particular reason to like each other, although, given the similar trajectories of their respective relationships with Stella, I can easily imagine the two of them exchanging mutual misogynistic commiserations!

First thing in the morning, I leave a phone message for DI Forrester informing him that I've belatedly remembered the identity of the person in the CCTV image taken at the bottom of Stella's road.

The detective sounds surprised when he calls me back. 'Are you certain it was him?'

'I think so. I thought he was vaguely familiar when you showed the video to me, but I was feeling too ill to think clearly at the time. I could look at the footage again if you like.'

'Yes, of course.'

He brings a copy of the video round for me to watch again, and I'm able to confirm that the man the camera caught striding along the bottom of Stella's road was indeed

Steve Cottram.

The detective's amazing eyebrows meet in a frown. 'In that case we'd better question Cottram again. He denied being in the area on the night of the party when we spoke to him.'

I give an involuntary shiver. Why did Steve Cottram lie about being in Stella's road on the night she was killed?

# Chapter 28

When DI Forrester calls on me again it's early in the morning and I'm rather put out as I'm in the middle of a delicate stage of my work on the book about children arriving on a planet. I take him into the kitchen rather than the living room and don't offer him coffee.

'Do you have any news?' I ask, washing the paint off my hands at the sink. 'Have you spoken to Steve Cottram again?'

'He's still being questioned.' Without waiting to be invited, the detective lowers himself onto a chair at the kitchen table.

I wait but as he doesn't disclose any more details, ask another question. 'Have you made any headway with the anonymous message?'

'Someone has been working on it.'

I feel irritated at the brevity of his replies and although I'm anxious to return to my work, sit down opposite him at the table. 'Have you asked Hugh Whitmore if he knows anything about it?'

'Yes. He denied having anything to do with it; he thought I must be pulling his leg to even ask him about it.'

I laugh. 'I'm not surprised. I can't see Hugh going to the trouble of cutting tiny pieces out of a paper to make an anonymous note.'

'Angela Robertson,' the detective announces abruptly. 'Do you know her?'

'Yes. What about her?'

'How well do you know her?'

'I knew her more when I was younger. She went to the same school as Stella and me. I've not had much to do with her since.'

He nods. 'Was she a friend of Stella's?'

I hesitate. 'Yes...and no.'

'What does that mean?'

'Well,' I reply cautiously, 'Angela... was ostensibly a friend of Stella's, but I think she was...rather jealous of her. There was a problem with a boyfriend, a long time ago. You know the kind of thing: Angela thought Stella had stolen him from her: teenage girl stuff.'

'That figures,' he says enigmatically.

'Why?'

He ignores the question. 'What about her husband?'

'Ian Robertson? What about him?'

'Was *he* a friend of Stella's?'

I wonder where this is leading. 'I don't think so. He was more a friend of Hugh's. He and Angela were at Hugh and Stella's wedding.'

'What about recently?'

I'm baffled. 'What do you mean?'

'What contact did Stella have with Ian Robertson after the divorce?'

'None as far as I know, or very little. I don't think she had much to do with either of them. Why?'

'But she asked them to her birthday party, didn't she?'

'She told me she'd put them on the guest list although

she said she didn't like Angela much. But I don't know whether they actually went to the party or not. I'm afraid I still can't remember anything about--'

'Did you know Stella had been seeing Ian Robertson?' The detective fixes me with a disconcerting gaze.

'What?'

'Were you aware that they were having an affair?'

I gasp. 'An affair? No! When?'

'During the period shortly before her party.'

'Are you sure?' Rigid with tension, I grip the edge of the table, wondering if there can be any more bombshells about Stella in store for me.

'Positive.'

'Who told you? How do you know they were having an affair?'

'Because the anonymous note, the one you found in Stella's bathroom, was sent by Ian Robertson's wife, Angela!'

'Angela? How do you know? How did you find out it was her?'

He smiles almost triumphantly. 'A mixture of forensic and detective work. Once the periodical the letters came from was identified – it was actually a weekly news magazine with a small circulation – and we discovered which of the party guests' households take that publication on a regular basis, it was just a matter of narrowing down. When the Robertsons were questioned, it didn't take long for Angela to admit it. She said she sent the message to Stella after she found out about the affair. She said she did it that way because she didn't think it could be traced back to her. She claims she didn't mean to *do* anything and she wasn't going to follow it up. It was just meant to frighten Stella; to warn her off. When she and Robertson received the party invitation, she confronted him about the affair.'

'Did he and Stella stop seeing each other after that?'

'I'm afraid not. So you weren't aware that Stella was having an affair with Ian Robertson?' the detective asks me again.

I swallow hard. 'Absolutely *not*. She never breathed a word about it to me.' I reflect that this is something I should be getting used to by now.

'No suspicion?'

'None at all.' But as I think back to the period immediately before Stella's party, something occurs to me. 'I do remember that Stella sometimes made excuses when I tried to arrange to see her on the evenings when we usually met. She said she was doing a facial or a massage for a friend at her home and would probably stay for a drink or a meal afterwards. I had no reason not to believe her.'

DI Forrester doesn't appear surprised.

I also recall something that Damian told me – that Hugh was "in cahoots with" Ian Robertson. In case this is relevant I add, 'Ian Robertson's Chair of the council planning committee so he and Hugh probably have interests in common. Damian Matthews implied they were pretty close. Is that significant do you think?'

The detective doesn't comment.

I feel suddenly apprehensive. 'What does this mean for the murder enquiry? Does it make any difference?'

His thick black brows knit together in a straight line. 'Well, it certainly adds a new dimension.' He glances at me. 'It seems more people were gunning for Stella than we originally thought.'

'You don't think Angela could have had something to do with what happened to Stella, do you?' Although I believe this is very unlikely I feel I have to ask the question. 'Do you think she could have confronted Stella about the affair at the party?'

'It's possible, although she says she didn't and no-one appears to have heard any arguments between them that night. You of course still can't remember…'

Although this is a statement rather than an accusation, I'm again overwhelmed with guilt, an all-too-familiar feeling these days.

My sense of trepidation increases. 'Do you think…Is it possible that Hugh Whitmore *wasn't* the one who killed Stella?'

He shakes his head. 'It's too early to come to that conclusion. Even if something did happen between Stella and Angela Robertson at the party, the Robertsons have a watertight alibi for later that night. Their babysitter says they got home around twelve twenty and Ian Robertson then drove her home, getting there well after half past midnight. CCTV confirms this. By the way, you're looking well, Hanna,' he adds, glancing at me as he rises to his feet.

I wonder why he's changed the subject so abruptly.

After he leaves I find it difficult to return to my work. I'm in a state of shock both at the discovery that Stella was having an affair with Ian Robertson and at the revelation that it was Angela who'd sent her the threatening note. I recall the detective hinting some time ago that Stella might have been having an affair before she died, but I dismissed the idea at the time. Did he know about it all along? Who else did? Did Hugh? How long had it been going on? Why didn't Stella tell me she was seeing Ian Robertson? Did she think I'd disapprove? I probably would have done. I picture the man – tall, burly, balding, rather red-faced – not Stella's usual type at all. On the other hand, he's smooth-tongued with an authoritative manner and certainly very well-off. Maybe those were the qualities that attracted her. Or perhaps, and this only strikes me now, because of the close connection between Ian and Hugh, she saw the affair as a way of getting back at her former husband. What is the answer? Stella whom I thought I knew so well, has become a complete enigma to me.

# Chapter 29

Since the detective's last visit I've been making a determined effort to dismiss Stella's affair with Ian Robertson from my mind. She's dead so what does it matter now? But of course it matters because it was something else she concealed from me during the last months of her life, and this once again brings into question the nature and depth of our friendship. Either because of this or the lingering impact of the head injury, I've been feeling rather strained and under the weather lately. In response, and to counteract the time I spend bending over my work, I've resolved to go for a long walk every day, despite plummeting temperatures as the end of autumn kicks in. To avoid monotony, I try to vary the direction of my walks and alternate between different routes.

Today's walk takes me down to the Old Steine and after passing Brighton Pavilion, I turn right. There's a busker at the top end of East Street, a young black woman wearing a bomber jacket and ripped jeans, and I stop to listen to her. She's singing in a deep smoky voice and accompanying herself on a guitar. It's the words of the song that arrest me. They're about poverty and homelessness.

*…How can you tell me you're lonely*

*And say for you that the sun doesn't shine*
*Oh, let me take you by the hand*
*And lead you through the streets of London*
*I'll show you something*
*To make you change your mind…*

Although I've heard the song many times before, it now holds a new significance for me. It wouldn't be difficult, I reflect, to replace London with Brighton or any other city in Britain in the late 2000s, come to that.

I glance at the other listeners standing around the singer and one face suddenly looms out at me. It belongs to Steve Cottram! Seeing him again is a shock. Our eyes briefly lock, and hoping that he hasn't recognised me, I hasten round the corner into North Street. But I've only progressed a few yards up the hill when I hear him hailing me and to my dismay, he catches me up.

I reluctantly come to a halt. 'Hello, Steve.'

'I thought it was you, Hanna.' He looks me up and down and smirks. 'Well! You've certainly changed, I must say, and for the better!'

'Pity I can't say the same for you!' I retort rudely. He's somewhat heavier than I remember and is now rather jowly, but he still has that cocky self-assurance I recall only too well.

I'm pleased to see a flicker of annoyance cross his face. He quickly converts it into an ingratiating smile that reminds me of why I disliked him so much in the past.

'I thought I saw you a while ago,' he comments. 'Coming out of *Sainsbury's* one evening, but I wasn't sure if it was you.'

'Oh?'

'Yeah, I called after you, but if it was you, you must have thought I was a mugger or something, because you made off like a bat out of hell! You disappeared round a corner and I didn't see where you went after that.'

I stare at him, recalling the terrifying occasion when I thought someone had followed me from the supermarket. 'That was *you*? You scared me half to death.'

He grins. 'Oh, sorry... I did call you but as you didn't answer, I assumed I was mistaken. You look ... different these days; thinner.'

'Why were you following me?'

'I needed to ask you something, about Regency Towers.'

'What's Regency Towers got to do with me?'

He doesn't answer. Instead, still wearing that annoying grin, he comments, 'I gather we have a mutual acquaintance.'

'Do we?'

'Yeah, Robbie Cole; young mixed-race guy; good-looking; says he's been staying with you.' Another smirk. 'Into toy boys these days, are you, Hanna?'

'Piss off, Steve!' I push past him but he follows, keeping in step beside me.

'Pity what happened to Stella, isn't it?' he mutters in an unbelievably casual way.

'*Pity?*' I stop walking and turn to face him. 'Stella was *murdered,* for Christ's sake. I can think of dozens of appropriate words to describe that – terrible, appalling, tragic, shocking, catastrophic... "A Pity" doesn't come anywhere near.' To my intense irritation, tears, always so near the surface these days, start to spill down my cheeks. I brush them away and try to dodge away from him up the hill, but within seconds he arrives by my side and again measures his pace to mine. 'Yeah, well,' he mutters, 'Stella had it coming to her if she went on acting with other guys like she did with me.'

I can't believe what I'm hearing and an explosion of rage sends the blood rushing to my face. Once again I stop walking and turn to confront him. 'Of course you'd approve of murdering a woman, wouldn't you, Steve? As I remember, domestic abuse was a speciality of yours.'

'You *remember*, do you, Hanna?' he says with another infuriating smirk. 'Are you sure you *remember*? I heard you're suffering from amnesia. Robbie Cole said you can't remember *anything* about the night Stella died; that's what you told him anyway, or have you been making it up? Have you really forgotten what happened that night?'

A shiver runs down my spine. Why is he asking me about that night? I decide to ignore the question and attack rather than defend. 'Was that why you went to Stella's flat after midnight on the night of her birthday party, Steve? To beat her up again?' (It's a long shot but worth a try).

His expression changes to one that's almost furtive, and realising that I've hit a nerve, I press my advantage. 'You see, CCTV took some pretty pictures of you at the bottom of the road where Stella lived.'

'So what?' he growls. 'There's no law against walking at night, is there?'

'Not that I know of, but why were you in Stella's road so late on the night she was killed?'

His face turns red with anger. 'I don't have to explain my movements to you.'

'No you don't, but you will have to explain them to the police.'

He gives an airy laugh. 'The police questioned me weeks

ago, and not just me; presumably all of Stella's exes. God knows the bitch had enough of them. And now that crook Whitmore's been charged, they won't need to speak to any of us again.'

I laugh in my turn. 'That's not the case. As you've been recognised in that CCTV footage, they will want to question you again. They'll want to find out exactly why you went to Stella's flat that night.' I turn away from him and continue up the hill.

'It was *you* who told them it was me in that video, wasn't it?' he calls after me. 'Fucking bitch!'

His use of the word "bitch" reminds me of the threatening message in Stella's bathrobe pocket, and I recall the detective's observation that there were more people than Hugh "gunning for" Stella. Was Steve Cottram another of them?

In yet another attempt to get away from him, I veer abruptly to the right and dart across the road, dodging between a pair of double-decker buses.

Shortly after I reach the opposite pavement, Steve reappears at my side, panting from the exertion of scurrying after me. I remember he used to keep fit by working out in a gym, but the extra weight he's accumulated seems to have slowed him down.

'Piss off and leave me alone!' I hiss at him.

Instead of following this instruction, he asks, 'What did Stella tell you about Whitmore, Hanna? What do you know about Regency Towers?'

'Nothing. I don't know anything about it.' I quicken my step without answering, but he still manages to keep alongside me and I begin to despair of shaking him off.

'Cole may have mentioned I used to live there,' he says,

his voice grating in my ear. 'Did he tell you I bought the penthouse flat? I paid a shedload of dosh for it; poured even more into getting it exactly how I liked it. Thanks to Whitmore, me and my partner had to move out but the insurance company's refusing to pay up. They're claiming non-compliance because he didn't comply with the conditions of the policy. He used cheap, shoddy materials; ignored safety procedures. Guy's an out-and-out crook. Thanks to him, I've bloody lost thousands!'

'Tough!' I hasten on up the hill but am obliged to slow down when I bump up against a large group of people blocking the pavement. As a result he catches me up again.

Putting a hand on my arm, a touch that makes me shrink away with distaste, he adopts a placatory tone. 'OK, I did go to Stella's flat that night, but you know that already, don't you, Hanna? It's no big deal. I wanted to confront Whitmore in person about what had happened. I've been trying to get hold of him ever since the Regency Towers balls-up. I went to his office once and nearly clocked him one, but I was ejected. After that I could never get hold of him; he ignored all my phone and email messages as well as solicitors' letters. I called Stella several times to find out if she had any info about his part in what happened but she wouldn't give me the time of day. Then she texted me out of the blue, very late that Saturday night, the night of her birthday party.'

I turn to stare at him. 'Stella texted you that night? Why would she do that?'

He blinks. 'She said if I wanted to confront Whitmore, he'd just fetched up there, at her flat. I was still up at the time, working online, so I rushed out, hoping to catch him.'

'And *did* you catch him?' I wonder how Stella felt on

seeing Steve again, years after their disastrous liaison.

Steve utters an angry snort. 'No. By the time I got there, he'd already left and the bitch just laughed at me. She was utterly wasted; pissed out of her fucking mind; she said she'd been looking forward to seeing two monsters duffing each other up.'

I'm astounded. What on earth had Stella been up to, and where was *I* when this happened? 'Did you see me when you were at the flat?' I ask him. 'The police say I was still there after the party ended, helping to clear up.'

He seems surprised. 'No, I didn't see you, you must know that. I only got as far as the door. Stella was standing on the pavement outside, giggling, the stupid bitch. She showed me the direction Whitmore had gone in and I went straight after him, but he must have driven away by then.'

'Did you tell the police about that when they questioned you?'

He hesitates. 'No.'

'Why not?'

His face turns a kind of puce colour. 'I was only there a few minutes so it didn't seem worth telling them.'

'Why not?'

'Why do you think? I couldn't face the hassle, especially as Stella was murdered that night, and her and me, we --'

'You mean she reported you for domestic abuse?'

'Yeah, well ... my partner doesn't know anything about that, and I'd rather she didn't hear about it.' His lip curls. 'Stella drove me to it. She was a bitch; a fucking--'

I don't want to hear any more so dive into the nearest shop and secrete myself behind a rail of sports clothing. I wait for a few moments but he doesn't follow me and I hope I've finally succeeded in losing him. When I leave the shop and look up and down the street, there's no sign of him.

The discovery that Steve went to Stella's flat after her party had ended intrigues me and as I continue on my walk, I reflect on his and Hugh's respective versions of events that night.

Hugh claims he went to the flat to give Stella a birthday present but says he left the flat because I was there and she'd had too much to drink. His story has, of course, been discredited.

Steve claims he went to the flat to confront Hugh about the financial losses he'd incurred because of the Regency Towers disaster, but he didn't actually go inside. If he is to be believed, he saw neither Hugh nor me that night, only Stella who was giggling tipsily, apparently hoping to witness an encounter between two of her former partners that would end in fisticuffs. But I only have his word for this. On balance, however, his story of wanting to catch up with Hugh seems plausible, particularly as I'd already heard about his animosity towards him from the detective and from Robbie. But…

My heart starts to pound as I belatedly realise something. If what Steve has told me is true, it means that Stella was *still alive* after Hugh had left the flat! The realisation leaves me so shaken that I come to an abrupt halt in the middle of the pavement. For a second time I question whether the right person has been charged with Stella's murder. What if it wasn't Hugh but *Steve Cottram*? When he went to Stella's flat that night, the front door was still open so he could easily have entered and attacked her. And if it was Steve who stabbed her, then he was also the one who attacked *me*. That would explain his interest in what I remember about that night and why he followed someone he thought was me from a shop one evening; it could have had nothing to do with finding out what Stella might have told me about Regency Towers. The thought that Robbie has, in all innocence, given him my address makes me go cold with fear.

But what motive could Steve have had for attacking Stella? Even though he'd been abusive towards her in the past and was out of his mind with rage when she left him, their relationship was some years ago and he now has a different partner.

My thoughts are in turmoil – Hugh, Damian, Steve, Ian and Angela Robertson – a jigsaw of connections in which the pieces fail to come together to make any meaningful sense. The only links seem to be the relationship each of them had with Stella.

I call DI Forrester and tell him what has happened. He assures me that the police have charged the right man but says that Steve's movements on the night of the murder will be investigated. 'The fact that he told us he was at home all night certainly brings his credibility into question.'

'But wasn't the text Stella sent him still on her phone?'

'No, she must have deleted it after it was delivered.'

He warns me not to mention what Steve has told me to anyone while the investigation is ongoing.

# Chapter 30

I haven't heard any more from the detective so am trying to carry on as normal despite the anxiety prompted by my encounter with Steve Cottram.

To calm my spirits and increase my general fitness level, in addition to my daily walks I've started going to an evening Yoga class. The members of the group are mostly women who are younger and far suppler than I am, but I persevere as it's not as strenuous as Zumba which I tried only once before staggering home afterwards, totally exhausted. The head injury has taken more out of me physically than I realised.

We're doing the customary short meditation at the end of one of the Yoga sessions, when I become aware of something different about my body – something I've been vaguely conscious of for a while but have ignored – a certain tightness in the breasts; an unusual feeling in the abdomen. Struck by a sudden suspicion, I do some rapid mental calculations and realise that I haven't had a period for nearly two months. As my periods have been erratic at the best of times, I haven't been over-concerned about this, but now my heart misses a beat. *Could* it be? As nothing happened after any of my previous sexual relationships and occasional unprotected one-night stands, I don't use the pill, and since

I started sleeping with Aidan, we've never discussed contraception. This now strikes me as odd, but I've never thought to bring the subject up and he has probably assumed I've been taking precautions.

First thing in the morning, I go to the nearest chemist and buy a pregnancy testing kit. I rush home and use it. As I suspected, the result is positive. I gaze at it with a mixture of conflicting emotions – exhilaration and apprehension, joy and terror. I'll soon be forty and at this stage in my life, I'm not sure whether to be happy or sorry. Although I used to long for a child, I'd come to the regretful conclusion that that I would never have one. I believed I was destined to turn into one of those old ladies I sometimes see on buses, gazing longingly at babies and small children with foolish smiles on their faces.

The father can only be Aidan, but how will he react when I tell him? If he panics and backs off, how will I manage? I just about scrape a living through my art, but can I afford to support a child as well as myself?

In the evening I call on Maria and confide my news. Though initially startled, she declares she's delighted on my behalf. 'That's wonderful!' she cries, embracing me. 'Have you told Aidan?'

'Not yet. I've only just found out myself.'

'But you are going to tell him?'

I hesitate. 'It's probably too soon. It might not even happen. Don't you think I'd better wait until it's more established?'

'Maybe.' She scrutinises me with a shrewd expression. 'You *are* pleased, aren't you?'

I hesitate before answering. 'I suppose so. I've always wanted a child but was resigned to never having one. I thought it was too late. I'm nearly forty after all. I'm …what's that awful term medics use for expectant mothers over 35? An Elderly Multigravida!'

Maria laughs. 'That's rubbish! I was over forty when I had George. But since you *are* an elderly whatsit, maybe you shouldn't be knocking back that double gin and tonic I poured you when you arrived!'

'Too late!' I flop down on her comfortable sofa and take a mouthful of the refreshing liquid. 'I need this to cushion the shock! This is absolutely the last thing I expected, Maria. I suppose that sounds crazy when I've been having unprotected sex with someone on a regular basis, but as I never got pregnant before, I assumed it would be the same this time.'

'Well, as long as you feel OK about it.' She passes me a bowl of peanuts. 'You *are* intending to go ahead with it, aren't you, Hanna?'

I'm surprised by the question as it hasn't once occurred to me to think about ending the pregnancy. 'Yes, of course I am.'

She beams. 'In that case, you know I'll be here to help when the time comes. But if I were you, I'd tell Aidan ASAP. He'll probably be delighted.'

'I will tell him,' I assure her, 'but only when I think the time's right.'

But when *will* the time be right? I wonder when I'm back in the solitude of my flat. Aidan and I have been lovers for such a short time. He's a decent, caring man and we get on very well, but isn't this far too early in our relationship? Is he ready for parenthood so soon after his divorce? More to the point, am *I* ready for it?

At Maria's prompting, I go to see my GP who confirms

the pregnancy. She refers me to the antenatal clinic at the health centre and says I should register there as soon as possible because of my age and because of my head injury which could create problems both before and after the birth. She assures me that this won't necessarily be the case, but says that to be on the safe side, I should start having check-ups immediately.

\* \* \*

Aware that the first months of pregnancy can be risky, I hug my secret to myself as the weeks pass. Maria is still the only person who knows and I've decided not to tell Aidan until the critical twelve-week period is up. Thanks to the regime of walking and Yoga, I'm now feeling reasonably fit and as far as I know, there's nothing about my appearance to alert anyone to my condition. My own attitude towards it, however, remains mixed: sometimes I experience an overwhelming sense of joy at the thought of having a child; at other times, usually in the middle of the night, I'm plunged into an abyss of anxiety at the possibility – if not likelihood– of having to cope as a single parent. It's a veritable seesaw of emotion which leaves me feeling confused.

# Chapter 31

When I arrive at the antenatal clinic for my first check-up, a woman in an advanced stage of pregnancy emerges from the building. It's Sarah, JC's wife.

'Hanna? What are you doing here?' She looks me up and down. 'No! Are you--?'

'Yes,' I feel myself blushing, 'but only a few weeks.'

'Aidan?'

'Yes, but he doesn't know yet. I'm waiting till it's more established.'

'Oh?' She seems surprised then smiles. 'Yes, I suppose that's wise.'

'How's yours going?' I eye her huge bump. It looks almost grotesque on someone so tiny.

She groans. 'Any day now…and the sooner the better.'

'Are you keeping well?'

'Yes, but it's so uncomfortable at this stage. I'm fed up with lumbering around like a beached whale.'

I must look alarmed for she adds quickly, 'It's been absolutely fine most of the time; no trouble at all; in fact it's been a doddle up to now, and I'm sure it'll be the same for you.'

'I hope so.'

She smiles and squeezes my hand. 'Of course it will. You

take care, Hanna.'

'By the way,' I say before she disappears into the car park, 'Nobody else knows about this yet except Maria, so please don't mention it to JC, Sarah, just in case… you know…'

She nods. 'I understand. You want to get through the first months before telling people, but I'm sure it'll go smoothly. Any morning sickness?'

'Not yet, thank goodness.' I wave goodbye as she waddles into the car park.

At the antenatal clinic I answer a number of questions on my general health and, as I expected, the head injury is noted as something that could cause concern. I'm told I can have my first ultrasound scan – the dating scan –between ten and fourteen weeks. Because of my age, I'm asked if I want it to include a nuchal translucency (NT) scan, part of the combined screening test for Downs syndrome. The possibility of having a Downs syndrome child has never occurred to me and inspires a whole new set of worries. Nevertheless I agree to have the NT scan as a precaution. I'm also advised to eat sensibly and take regular exercise.

Not long after my encounter with Sarah, morning sickness ironically becomes an unwelcome daily occurrence. It's a scourge but, as I work from home, a manageable one. However it sometimes has a knock-on effect on my ability to sustain late nights and I occasionally don't feel well enough to accompany Aidan on outings at weekends. As a result, I have to make excuses for not seeing him as often as usual. He's concerned but assumes I'm indisposed because of my habitual headaches. He rings every day to ask how I am and frequently calls round on his way back from work in the evenings. We continue to spend weekend nights together and since there's nothing so far to reveal that I'm pregnant, he doesn't seem to suspect. But I realise it won't be long before my condition starts to show. I'm only too aware of the irony: having acquired a slim figure for the first time in my adult life, I'm about to put weight back on again!

The combination of morning sickness and keeping up with my work distracts me from brooding on the potential impact of what I have learnt from Steve Cottram on the murder enquiry and Hugh's arrest. But there's always a tight knot of anxiety at the back of my mind which threatens to unravel and overwhelm me at any moment. As the pregnancy progresses, however, I'm beset by a host of more immediate worries: will Aidan still be attracted to me when I'm waddling around looking as huge as Sarah does now? What if he thinks I deliberately became pregnant in order to trap him and fix our relationship in cement? He might drop me and disappear completely from my life, leaving me bereft. If that happens, will I be able to cope as a single mother on my self-employed income?

Other more practical issues start to niggle at me: will my tiny flat be suitable for a small child? Although it's big enough to accommodate a baby, it will be very cramped once that baby grows into an active toddler, and the block has no outdoor space for children to play in. But on the whole my excitement at the prospect of having a child overrides these concerns and I begin to make a few modest plans. When the first three months are up, I'll buy a carrycot to put next to my bed and a colourful mobile to hang in front of it so that the baby will have something stimulating to look at. I'll also start to acquire the necessary baby clothes and equipment but am not sure what to get. I do an online search and download a list of the stuff a newborn is likely to need. It's terrifyingly long!

* * *

One morning I receive a text message from JC to say that Sarah has had another boy whom they've named Eliot. When I call round at the weekend with a small present for the baby, Sarah is having a much needed nap and JC, beaming with pride, takes me into the tiny room they use as a nursery where Eliot is lying in his cot. He has a crumpled red face and a shock of dark hair. He peers up at me with a rather worried expression as though he's trying to work out who I am.

My insides melt. 'He's adorable,' I tell JC.

JC grins happily. 'I can't disagree, though he tends to lose a bit of adorableness every time he wakes us during the night!'

Eliot's older siblings tiptoe into the room to join us. They both gaze down at their baby brother, Scarlett with a fond smile on her face, whereas Josh looks rather unimpressed.

When I leave the house, JC gives me a searching look. 'What about you, Hanna? Are you going to start a family soon? Don't leave it too late.'

I feel myself blush and mutter something non-committal. Sarah has obviously kept her promise and not mentioned my pregnancy, but I wonder if he's noticed something different in my appearance. If he has, I feel I can't tell JC before I've informed Aidan that he's going to become a father.

# Chapter 32

DI Forrester has called round. He gives me an appraising look followed by a knowing smile. I wonder if he's guessed that I'm pregnant. He doesn't make any comment, however, and after taking his usual chair in the kitchen, he informs me that re-examination of CCTV footage has confirmed Steve's story of trying to catch up with Hugh.

'The camera caught him at the top of the road near where Whitmore's *Lexus* had been parked, but Whitmore had already driven away by then. He wandered around for a few seconds then disappeared out of the camera's reach. The timing between his being caught on CCTV walking along the bottom of Stella's road, then at the top, was no more than fifteen minutes.'

I breathe a sigh of relief. 'That wouldn't have given him time to enter the flat, stab Stella, attack me, then wash the skillet.'

'No, it wouldn't.'

'But couldn't he have gone back to the flat after he went looking for Hugh?'

'There's no evidence of that. Later CCTV footage from near the bottom of Stella's road where the first camera caught him, indicates that he retraced his steps less than ten minutes after trying to catch up with Whitmore. He's still being questioned and he insists he didn't go back to the flat.' He drums pensively on the kitchen table with his fingers. 'And I'm inclined to believe him. After all, what motive would he have had, given that his relationship with Stella was so long ago? Do you have a view?'

'I can't think of a motive, unless he was still pissed off with her for leaving him. But it seems a long time to bear that kind of grudge.'

The detective nods. 'I agree. It's not very plausible, especially as he's now with another partner. On the other hand, his grievance about Regency Towers is perfectly understandable. He spent a lot of money on the penthouse flat but hasn't managed to secure any compensation. As the owner of the freehold, Whitmore was responsible for arranging buildings insurance for the property as a whole, but his insurers are refusing to pay up on the grounds that he must have given his contractors specifications regarding the materials used. If he deliberately chose inferior ones, the insurers are within their rights to withhold payment.'

'Yes, Steve told me that.' I take a deep breath and ask the question that has been preying on my mind. 'But if he's telling the truth, what does it mean for the investigation?'

The detective slowly flexes and unflexes his fingers before replying.

'Cottram's evidence will need to be properly evaluated of course, but if it turns out to be accurate — if Stella *was* still alive after Whitmore left the building — I'm afraid it will put an entirely new slant on things.'

I catch my breath. 'Meaning?'

'*If* it's accurate – and we don't know yet for sure whether it is or not– then we'll have to apply for a discontinuance notice.'

'What's that?'

'It means we'll have to inform the Crown Prosecution Service that on the basis of newly available evidence, Whitmore won't be charged and therefore proceedings will be terminated before he goes to trial. He'll be advised that he can be released immediately.'

I go cold. 'But that would mean whoever killed Stella could still be at large.'

'I'm afraid so.' He clears his throat. 'If it does come to the point where Whitmore has to be released, as you're a key witness we can apply for you to be placed under formal protection.'

I gasp. 'What will that involve?'

'There's no need to worry about that just yet. I'll let you know in due course after we've fully investigated Cottram's story.'

I groan. 'I didn't think I needed to be worried about my own safety once Hugh was taken into custody.'

He looks apologetic. 'That's understandable and I'm sorry the case has turned out to be less straightforward than we thought. But as I say, if we find Cottram's evidence is true and Whitmore's released, we should be able to arrange a protection package for you. I'll keep you in the loop of course. In the meantime...' He eyes me rather sternly '...I must ask you again to say nothing about this to anyone, Hanna, as it could compromise the enquiry. We may still have charged the right person and we don't want to jump any guns...not just yet.'

After accompanying him to the door, I collapse onto a chair feeling totally shattered. Just as I was beginning to achieve a more settled frame of mind, the nightmare has returned. But there's nothing I can do about it and to distract myself from anxious thoughts, I decide to concentrate on the momentous event occurring in my life.

* * *

The morning sickness has finally receded and Maria accompanies me to the antenatal clinic for the dating and NT scan.

It turns out to be a memorable day. When the sonographer puts gel on my stomach and moves a hand-held device over it, Maria grabs my hand and we both gaze, enthralled, at the swirly grey image on the ultrasound screen. In it I can just about make out a minuscule curved form, shaped like a tadpole or a prawn, with a head that's considerably larger than the tiny limbs. The sight moves me almost to tears.

I'm informed that the baby is developing well, its heartbeat is fine and there's no sign of any abnormalities. This is a huge relief. I don't know yet whether it's a boy or a girl but am told I can find this out when I come for the next scan, which will be at around twenty weeks.

I'm given a photo of the scan to take home with me.

Maria is beaming from ear to ear as we walk to the bus stop. 'There you are! Aren't you excited?'

'Yes, of course I am. It's such a relief to know there's a real baby in there. It felt like a dream before.'

'So when are you going to tell Aidan?'

'As soon as possible now that I know the baby's OK. I'd better tell him before he notices the weight start piling on.'

Maria squeezes my hand. 'He'll be fine with it, you'll see.'

'Yes, I expect so,' I murmur without certainty. 'I've

arranged to meet him in an Italian restaurant on Thursday evening.'

# Chapter 33

I have flutters of apprehension as I make my way to the restaurant.

Unfortunately the evening gets off to a bad start. The establishment is crowded and the volume of noise combined with my nervousness renders our conversation uncharacteristically stilted. Aidan also seems slightly edgy and we lapse into an awkward silence when the waiter brings us our meals. Aidan assumes I'm not drinking wine because I'm still unwell, and eyes me anxiously as I push my pasta around the plate with my fork.

'Are you OK, Hanna?' he asks eventually. 'You're very pale. Are you still feeling under the weather?'

I bestow on him what I hope is a reassuring smile. 'No, I'm fine.' Which of course is far from the truth. I'm actually almost paralysed with anxiety and am finding it difficult to eat.

'Are you still having headaches?'

'No,' I reassure him, 'really, I'm fine. But I have a surprise for you. I hope you'll like it.'

He looks at me questioningly. 'Oh? What is it?'

I decide to wait for a quiet moment before dropping my bombshell. 'I'll tell you in a minute.'

He looks intrigued and as soon as the noise level drops, I

rummage in my bag, produce the envelope containing the precious photo of the scan and hold it out to him.

'What's this?' He puts down his knife and fork and taking the envelope, stares at it in surprise.

'Take a look at what's inside.'

'He extracts the photo and gazes at it uncomprehendingly for a second, then his eyes widen. 'Is this…what I think it is?'

'What do you think it is?'

'A scan…a foetus…'

'Yes.'

He gasps, peers again at the photo then looks up at me. 'It's *your* scan? *You're* pregnant?'

'Yes.'

'Is this is why you've been so off-colour lately?'

'Yes.' I hold my breath then blurt, 'It's yours of course.'

He's silent and I notice his mouth twitching as though he's experiencing a fierce emotion. I fear the worst and all my muscles tense as I await his reaction. But then his face breaks into a wide beam. He reaches across and grabs one of my hands. 'That's wonderful!'

'Is it?' I can scarcely believe what I'm hearing. 'Do you think so? You don't mind?'

'*Mind?*' If anything his smile stretches even wider. 'Of course I don't mind! I couldn't be happier, Hanna, I'm delighted.' He reaches across the table and grips my hand so tightly it hurts. 'It's the best news I've had in ages! I never thought… never dreamed… I always wanted children but Joanna didn't… she wouldn't… Well, I've already told you about that.' He's almost stammering with emotion. 'It's wonderful news. We must have a drink to celebrate. Oh no!' He shakes his head. 'You can't, can you? I understand why now.'

I begin to relax, unbelievably relieved. I couldn't have wished for a better reaction.

He stares again at the photo of the scan. 'How long?'

'It's due in about six months – around the end of May.'

He peppers me with questions: how I'm feeling; what I've been told at the antenatal clinic; whether the baby is developing satisfactorily.

'Do you know what sex it is?' he asks after I've exhausted all I can remember of what I was told at the clinic.

'Not yet. But they'll be able to tell when I have the next scan, at twenty weeks.'

The waiter hovers by our table. Although we've scarcely touched our meals, it must look as though we've finished eating. Aidan waves him away. After studying the photo again, he replaces it carefully in the envelope and hands it back to me. He looks thoughtful and for a bleak moment I wonder if he's revising his initial reaction.

'Well,' he says eventually, 'we should start making plans. You'll need to take things easy from now on, Hanna. You'll have to move in with me--'

'Move in with you?' Although I've been hoping we might have a future together, the idea of immediately sharing a home with Aidan hasn't occurred to me. 'No, it's far too soon for that.'

'Hanna! You'll need taking care of.'

I laugh. 'And how do you think you're going to do that when you're out all day? I'm perfectly comfortable living where I am for the time being. After all, the work I do isn't exactly strenuous.'

His face falls. 'But your place is tiny. I've got far more room than you.'

'I know you have, but there's plenty of time to think about that. It's early days; I'm only about twelve weeks gone.'

He considers for a moment then says, 'I suppose you're right. We can decide early next year.'

Relieved that the decision has been temporarily shelved, I pick up my fork and start eating my neglected *linguine alle vongole*. Now that he's reacted so positively to my news, my appetite has returned with a vengeance.

Aidan's in high spirits as we continue our meal and persuades me to have one small glass of champagne. He tips the waiter lavishly when we leave and calls a taxi although I'd prefer to walk home like we usually do. He doesn't stay the night at mine as he has to leave early for work in the morning, and when we part, he makes me promise repeatedly to take proper care of myself.

I go to bed feeling considerably happier than I was earlier in the evening. My worries about the impact of Steve Cottram's version of events on the murder enquiry have receded, and when I resume work on my illustrations in the morning, I'm in a very contented state of mind.

I'm amazed when the doorbell rings and a large bouquet of red roses is delivered to me. It's from Aidan. This is the first time a man has ever sent me flowers, and although I used to scoff at the importance Stella attached to such niceties, I'm both touched and delighted. The printed message on the card reads, *Thank you for giving me the best news ever, Aidan XX*

It's only when I remove the roses from their wrapping paper that I notice with a jolt that they come from the same florist shop as the bouquet of red roses I saw in the Garden of Remembrance. Could it have been Aidan who left it by

Stella's plaque, together with the message that she would be "forever loved"? The thought inspires a fierce pang of jealousy for which I immediately feel guilty. It can't be right to feel jealous of someone who's dead, can it?

'What did I tell you?' says Maria after I show her the flowers and describe how the evening went. 'I knew Aidan would be delighted. And maybe you *should* move in with him.'

'Maria! Are you trying to get rid of me?'

'Of course not, but don't you think it would be more practical? He's got a whole house. You've only got two rooms, not counting the kitchen and that cupboard you do your work in. And believe me, babies grow very fast.'

'I don't want to move in with him, not yet anyway. It's too early. Maybe I will nearer the time or once the baby's here.' As I say this, I realise that I don't really like Aidan's rather dark, north-facing and sparsely furnished house. He's already none too pleased that I'm not spending Christmas there with him, but with my sister and her family in Birmingham. The arrangement was made some time ago, before he and I got together, and as I visit my sister so rarely, I don't feel I can change it.

Now that Aidan knows about the pregnancy, I no longer feel the need to conceal my condition from others. I tell JC when I see him and Robbie when I call to invite him to join Maria and myself for a meal. Both are delighted on my behalf. JC offers to pass on some of the stuff Eliot will have grown out of when my baby arrives, and Robbie declares that Aidan is a very lucky man.

# Chapter 34

I lie listening to the gentle pattering of rain on the window. I feel too comfortable to get up and now that I'm pregnant, I have an excuse to rise later than usual in the mornings. The sound of my phone ringing in the living room, however, forces me reluctantly out of bed.

'It's DI Forrester. I thought you'd like to know that Cottram's story is still being investigated, so Hugh Whitmore is remaining in custody, at least for the time being.'

'But what if you find out that he didn't murder Stella? The killer could still be out there, and he may try to stop me identifying him.'

'We don't yet have any evidence of that, Hanna. And as I told you before, we can put you under witness protection if necessary.'

Although I appreciate that this is meant to reassure me, it doesn't lessen my unease at the possibility that Hugh might eventually be released. However my anxiety is quickly replaced by another more pressing one, for when I'm making my bed, I notice there are spots of blood on the sheet. I hope it's just a one-off, but as the day goes on, the bleeding restarts, then intensifies. Although the critical twelve-week period has already passed, I'm terrified in case

I'm having a miscarriage.

I call Maria who rushes home and drives me to A and E and I end up in the same hospital where I was before, but this time in a unit of the maternity department.

Maria contacts Aidan on my behalf but he's unable to get home in time for normal visiting hours. He sends a series of frantic messages to my mobile, to which I respond with assurances that I'm OK and in the right hands. He says he'll come to the hospital as soon as he can.

I'm examined by doctors and after a series of tests, they conclude that the bleeding is caused by a polyp that can be removed after the birth. The bleeding eventually stops but I'm kept in for observation as I have high blood pressure and they fear there could be complications related to the head injury.

I'm surprised when Robbie turns up in the unit late on Friday afternoon. He'd heard about my hospitalisation from Maria when she rang to cancel the meal the three of us had arranged. He sits and chats with me for a while and before he leaves, gives me a small piece of crystal quartz which he says has powerful healing properties. I clutch the crystal tight in my hand, willing it to do its magic and ensure that the baby is safe and healthy.

Aidan visits me at the weekend. He bends to kiss me before sinking onto the chair next to my bed and gripping my hand. 'I've been out of my mind with worry; I was terrified you might lose the baby. I'm so relieved you're both OK.'

'We're both fine.' I reassure him, touched by his concern. 'It was just a polyp, nothing serious.'

'Thank God for that. Do you know when you'll be discharged?'

'They want to keep me for another day or two, just to be on the safe side. Apparently I just need to rest.'

'Quite right,' he declares. 'I thought you were overdoing it with all that walking and Yoga. Didn't I say you needed looking after?'

'Don't worry. Maria's determined to keep an eye on me when I get home.'

To distract him from obsessing about my health, I tell him about the lists of baby clothes and equipment I've made, and he offers to contribute towards their cost. Although I thank him I have no intention of accepting. For some perverse reason I don't understand, I'm reluctant to share the enjoyment of making preparations for the baby with him; at least for the moment.

'I think you should reconsider,' he says, 'about moving in with me till the baby's born.'

I find myself prevaricating. 'I'll decide later, in the New Year like you suggested. Let's see how it goes. And you needn't worry. Maria says she'll be around to give me a hand if I need anything.'

With an air of disappointment, he picks up the crystal quartz on my locker and peers at it. 'What's this?'

'It's a piece of crystal quartz. Robbie gave it to me. He says it has powerful healing qualities.'

'Robbie?' Aidan's expression darkens. 'You mean that rough sleeper guy you put up?'

'Yes, he came to see me. Wasn't that nice of him?' I realise too late that I've made a mistake mentioning Robbie given Aidan's hostility towards him. 'He's not homeless anymore. He's working now and has a room at--'

'You mean he came to visit you, *here*?' Aidan's tone is incredulous.

'Yes, why not? Maria told him what had happened and he was worried about me.'

'So you're still in contact with him?'

'Yes.'

'You *see* him?'

'Yes, occasionally. He's a friend.' I don't mention that since he moved into his current accommodation, Robbie and I talk frequently on the phone and he occasionally joins Maria and me for our fortnightly meal out. I know this wouldn't go down well as Aidan has a strong streak of jealousy.

'A *friend?*' Aidan doesn't comment further. Instead he starts humming quietly to himself and I notice a range of expressions chase themselves across his face: anger, doubt and bewilderment. Finally he summons a forced smile, fumbles in a pocket and mutters, 'Well I've got something for you too.' He produces a small box wrapped in gift paper and hands it to me.

'For me?'

'Yes, a little something to thank you for giving me what I've always wanted; for being the mother of my child.'

'Thank you.' I feel slightly uneasy, although superstitious might be a more appropriate word as I'm not *yet* a mother. I stare at the little box then tear off the wrapping paper. Inside is a small black jewel box. Opening it, I stare, horrified, at what it contains: a beautiful diamond pendant...*in the shape of a rose.*

I raise my head and find Aidan watching me expectantly. He's smiling, but it's a strange smile. 'Well, what do you think? Do you like it? I chose it specially.'

Before I can respond, we're informed that visiting time is over and people who aren't patients are shooed out of the unit by a nurse. Aidan blows me a kiss and leaves.

I look down at the pendant in my hand and there's a kind of explosion in my skull.

Suddenly *I know; I remember.*

# Chapter 35

It's after midnight and the guests are clustered around Stella, thanking her and kissing her goodbye. I'm feeling tired and wish they would speed up their leave-taking, but they trickle out of the living room into the hall with agonising slowness, some more steady on their feet than others. Stella herself is somewhat the worse for wear, having consumed God knows how many glasses of champagne. But why not? I ask myself. It's her fortieth birthday after all; the only fortieth birthday she'll ever have.

As soon as the last stragglers have left, I start collecting up the plates and drinking glasses strewn around the room and pile them onto a tray. I can hear Stella speaking to someone outside so assume one of the guests is still lingering. After a few minutes she comes into the living room accompanied by a man and to my astonishment and dismay, I see that it's...Hugh Whitmore of all people! What's he doing here at this time of night and why on earth has she invited him in?

He glances at me with a rather embarrassed expression and mutters, 'Hello, Hanna.'

I don't deign to reply.

Avoiding my eye, Stella leads him into the kitchen where they continue to converse in low voices.

Intrigued, I continue with the clearing up and when the tray is loaded, I follow them into the kitchen and put the dirty plates and glasses on one of the worktops. They immediately fall silent. I wonder what they've been talking about and why Stella is giving this man the time of day after all she endured during the marriage and the bitterly contested divorce. I shoot a questioning glance at her but she ignores it. When I return to the living room with the empty tray, I'm annoyed to hear the kitchen door click shut behind me. What is it that they don't want me to hear?

Their voices are now raised but I can't make out what they're saying.

I make several return trips to the kitchen with a loaded tray and each time there is the same sequence: Stella and Hugh fall silent while I, deliberately slowly, place the dirty plates and cutlery in the dishwasher and the glasses on the worktop beside the sink. When I go back to the living room, one of them immediately shuts the door firmly behind me.

Eventually Stella follows me out of the kitchen. When I try to question her, she brushes past me saying she's going to get Hugh some champagne. Before she pours him a glass, however, I see her rapidly send a text from her mobile. She puts the phone down, pours two glasses from an opened bottle of champagne on the sideboard and takes them back to the kitchen, shutting the door behind her.

A minute or so later her phone beeps. On an impulse I pick it up and am amazed see a text message from Steve Cottram! *Steve Cottram –Stella's erstwhile lover and abuser?*

All it says is "*coming*".

I know Stella's password so check the text she sent before. It was to Steve. "*hugh w is at my flat now if u want to catch him.*"

I'm astounded. What on earth is going on? Why has Stella been contacting Steve Cottram? Her relationship with him was years ago. And why does she want him to come here and catch Hugh? Why isn't she keeping me in the picture? On an impulse I angrily delete both text messages.

I again hear raised voices in the kitchen. It sounds as though Stella and Hugh are arguing. After about ten minutes, the two of them come out of the kitchen and I assume with some relief that he's leaving. As they pass through the living room into the hall, Stella doesn't look at me and Hugh's expression is blank. Their voices recede and after a minute or two when I glance into the hall, I notice that the front door is open. Hearing Stella's occasional peals of rather strident laughter in the distance, I realise that she's speaking to Hugh on the pavement outside. I wish she'd hurry up and come back in so I can ask her what's been going on. By now I'm feeling extremely impatient. Although I would love to find out why Hugh has come, why she's tolerated his visit, and what the text messages between her and Steve Cottram were all about, I desperately want to go home and get to bed. As I expected, I've found the party quite stressful, although I've done everything Stella required of me: circulated with plates of food; topped up people's glasses; made polite small talk to people I don't particularly like.

I take another tray-load into the kitchen and am cramming a few more plates into the dishwasher when I hear voices coming from the living room. Going to the door, I see Stella in there with a man, but to my astonishment, this time it isn't Hugh: it's Aidan Miller – Stella's long-term admirer and one of the guests I thought had left the flat some time ago. Maybe he'd remained outside, waiting for everyone else to leave. He's red-faced and his manner seems rather excitable. Like Stella, he's probably imbibed a bit too much alcohol over the course of the evening. Stella herself is giggling and swaying slightly on her feet.

I catch fragments of their exchange and gather that Aidan is asking her questions about Hugh Whitmore and Steve Cottram.

'None of your business,' Stella retorts. 'Go home, Aidan. The party's over.' She pours herself another glass of champagne from the bottle on the sideboard and totters past me into the kitchen.

Ignoring me, Aidan follows her.

Although I move tactfully into the living room I can't help overhearing some of their conversation as the door is still ajar.

Aidan's voice: 'Why are you still seeing those bastards after all they--'

'None of your bloody business!'

'What did Whitmore give you when you were outside?' he demands. 'Show me!'

Stella's reply is inaudible and after a few seconds of angry-sounding muttered exchanges, I hear Aidan ask, 'Why the fuck are you taking presents from that bastard after the way he acted?'

*What* "presents"? To hear better, I move closer to the kitchen door. What Aidan says next makes me gasp.

'There's a rumour that you've been seeing Ian Robertson. Is it true?'

I'm stunned. Ian Robertson, Angela's husband, is a close friend of Hugh's. What's Aidan talking about?

Stella laughs -- a rather unpleasant, mocking sound – but doesn't answer.

'Say it's not true!' Aidan insists.

'It's none of your fucking business.' Stella's voice has become shrill.

'Tell me it's not true!' Aidan sounds almost hysterical. 'What the hell are you doing, Stella? Robertson's a married man. Why are you bothering with those sleazebags when I could offer you...' His voice drops and he appears to be pleading with her but I can only manage to catch odd words: 'Why?... We're both free ... You and I ...We could...'

'I've told you a thousand times, Aidan, I'm *not* interested. Go home. Leave me alone.'

I sigh. Surely Aidan must know by now that he doesn't stand a chance with her.

'Why are you being like this?' Aidan's voice is getting louder; insistent. 'Why don't you give it a go? You must know--'

'Oh fuck off, Aidan! Party's over and I'm tired.'

'I'm not going to fuck off!'

'Let go of me!'

One of them pushes the kitchen door shut with a bang but I can still just about hear their voices. Aidan's alternately shouting and pleading and Stella's yelling back at him. She sounds incoherent.

Exasperated, I decide to go home. I haven't finished clearing up the living room but as Stella is once again closeted inside the kitchen with a man and obviously not in a fit state to assist, she'll just have to do the rest of it herself when she gets up later in the morning. I'll call her at midday and jolly well make her tell me what Hugh was doing here, and what Aidan meant about her and Ian Robertson.

I go and fetch my jacket from the hall. Just as I'm putting it on, I hear scuffling noises then a loud thud from the kitchen. Stella screams, not once but several times. I drop the jacket and run and open the door. For what seems like an eternity I stand there, paralysed with shock. Stella's lying on the kitchen floor and there's a red stain spreading through her lovely white dress. Aidan's bending over her. He seems to be humming. He turns, grabs something from a worktop, and bounds towards me.

# Chapter 36

When DI Forrester and a female colleague come to take a statement, the detective makes a rather feeble joke about once again questioning me in a hospital bed. I don't find it funny. He tries to make me feel better by telling me that I should feel more secure now that they have finally charged "the right man". But why does the "right" man have to be *my* man; the one I fell in love with?

After the abrupt return of my memory, I sobbed, no, *howled*, with the pain of discovering that the man I loved – the father of my child – was the one who had murdered my best friend and left me for dead. I ricocheted between a whole gamut of draining emotions – shock, disbelief, anger, bitterness and despair. I couldn't sleep and refused to eat. I lost interest in the pregnancy and wouldn't cooperate with medical staff. They insisted on keeping me in hospital, as much for the baby's sake as for my own, and I was moved into a separate area where I wouldn't upset other expectant mothers.

Now all I feel is numb. At times I wish that my memory of what happened that night hadn't returned.

Aidan has tried to contact me from prison several times. He sent me a long message saying he's truly sorry for what he did to Stella and me, but claiming he was drunk at the time and not in his proper mind. It was "completely out of character". That will be his defence, I imagine. He said he hoped I can forgive him for what he did and insisted he cared for me and was genuinely thrilled at the prospect of becoming a father. He asked me to send him news of the baby as soon as it's born and begged me to allow him to have some contact with the child as it grows.

I didn't respond and deleted his number from my phone. I wish I could delete him as easily from my mind and from my heart. Although the thought is almost too painful to bear, I suspect that he only sought me out and initiated our relationship in order to keep a close watch on me in case I remembered what happened on the night of the party and could identify him. I'm forced to conclude that his interest in me was just a charade and the alleged solicitude about my health, worthy of an Oscar.

Questions spiral endlessly in my head. What was he planning to do if and when my memory returned? Did he intend to try and kill me a second time? Or was he banking on the possibility that it would never return? And what if it returned after the baby was born and we were living together? Would he try to kill me then – the mother of his child?

The mistake Aidan made was that he thought I wasn't aware of the pendant. He knew I hadn't seen it because I was still inside the flat when Hugh gave it to Stella. and I was unconscious when he took it off her in the kitchen. He didn't know I'd been given a description of the pendant by the detective, and luckily, I'd never thought to mention it to him.

When I think back, there were a number of signs indicating that Aidan was in a strange and confused state of mind during the months that followed Stella's death: his troubled demeanour whenever she was mentioned; his continuing attempt to elevate her to an ideal, even after he'd killed her; the bouquet of roses he left in the Garden of Remembrance; the night he called out Stella's name when we were making love, and his fierce jealousy of her former partners and lovers, a jealousy that extended even to me, as if I was a surrogate for her. I was aware of all of this, of course, but any misgivings I may have subconsciously felt were obliterated by the overwhelming physical attraction I felt for him. In my calmer moments, I can almost feel sorry for him for never achieving the object of his desire. Maybe he thought our child was going to be a substitute for Stella – someone on whom he could lavish the love he'd had for her, and who would return that love in equal measure. On the other hand, his preparedness to allow others to take the blame for his actions reveals an ugly side to him I never suspected and which I find repugnant.

I realise that there will be problems ahead. Will Aidan have parental rights even if he gets a life sentence? And what will I tell our child when he or she asks about their father? Shall I prevaricate and, like Mr and Mrs Knight, wait for his/her sixteenth birthday before revealing the unpleasant truth? There are no easy answers to these questions so I decide to shelve them until I'm in a more settled frame of mind.

After I'm discharged from the Maternity Unit, I go to my sister's in Birmingham.

# Chapter 37

Maria meets me at the station. I've been away for several weeks as I couldn't face coming back to Brighton straight after Christmas. My sister Penny urged me to stay with her and her family for longer, even until the birth, but I couldn't stay away from home indefinitely. I have work on a book to complete and need to continue my check-ups at the antenatal clinic.

As Maria drives me home, she tells me that a number of friends have been enquiring after me, including Robbie who, she says, is now volunteering for a few hours a week at a new hostel for the homeless, helping with maintenance issues.

In my flat, I find a card with a message from JC and Sarah, offering me their love and support. I'm touched by their kindness. There's also a note enclosed in a Christmas card from Mr and Mrs Knight. The message says they'd heard about Aidan's arrest from their family liaison officer and they're relieved that the real culprit has finally been charged. I don't know whether they've been told about my relationship with Aidan or my pregnancy. I hadn't been in a fit state to send any Christmas card messages myself.

DI Forrester comes to see me a few days after I've settled back and asks me to check through my statement to see if I wish to change or add anything. I find this difficult as it's excruciatingly painful to relive the details of what happened to Stella after the party.

After I've made a few minor amendments, the detective announces rather cautiously that I may have to testify against Aidan in court.

I'm horrified at the idea. 'Shouldn't my statement be enough to prove that it was him?'

'It should be,' he says, 'but it will depend on how he pleads. If he pleads guilty, you won't have to go to court or give evidence. Your statement will just be read out in court. But if he pleads not guilty and claims some mitigating circumstances, then you may have to testify in person. Although …' he eyes my baby bump which has now expanded to the point where it's extremely visible '…you may have mitigating circumstances of your own that will prevent you from going to court. It could take a while before the case comes up of course.'

'I don't care how long it takes. I just hope I won't have to give evidence.'

'That's perfectly understandable. But I need to ask you about something else, Hanna. It's about the diamond pendant. As you know, it's going to be used as evidence in the trial and as it was originally given to Stella it would normally be returned to her next of kin after the trial is over. However her parents say they don't want it.'

'I'm not surprised in the circumstances!'

'Apparently they want *you* to have it,' he tells me. 'It's a very expensive item.'

'*Me?*' I shudder at the thought. 'It's the last thing I want. It would just remind me of Aidan and how Stella died.'

'Well that's what they want.'

'In that case,' I say after a moment of reflection, 'I'll sell it and give the proceeds to a charity for the homeless.'

He nods approvingly.

'What about Hugh Whitmore?' I ask him. 'I assume he's been released?'

'Yes he has, but he now faces a charge of corruption under the *Bribery Act*. It turns out that he's been paying Ian Robertson backhanders for years.'

'Backhanders?'

'Yes. He's been paying him large sums of money to persuade the local planning committee to push through *Whitmore Futures* developments despite any local concerns or objections regarding location and safety. Regency Towers was only one case in point.'

'That doesn't surprise me. How did you find out?'

'From Angela Robertson when we questioned her about the anonymous message. By then we knew that her husband had continued the affair with Stella even after she'd confronted him about it, and when Angela heard this, she "sang like a canary", to use a phrase popular in crime fiction, in order to get her revenge.' He smiles at my grunt of surprise. 'When we re-questioned Whitmore, he admitted that Stella's threat to blackmail him wasn't about his negligence in relation to Regency Towers; it was actually to expose his financial dealings with Ian Robertson. Stella managed to extract the truth from Robertson during their affair. But as it happens, she wasn't a very effective blackmailer. She was too drunk that night to carry through her plan and Whitmore was convinced that his expensive birthday present – which he gave her before he drove away that night – had disarmed her to the point where she was prepared to drop the idea, at least temporarily.'

What will happen to him and Ian Robertson?' I ask after absorbing this information.

He smiles. 'Whitmore could get up to ten years in prison for the offence and a large fine. His company will be wound up. Robertson has also committed an offence by accepting bribes in performance of a public office so he'll also be charged. And of course he'll lose his position on the council.'

For Stella's sake I feel a strong sense of satisfaction that Hugh isn't going to escape prosecution. Even though she didn't carry out her threat of blackmail, she has succeeded in taking her revenge on him. Perhaps that was her goal in having the affair with Ian Robertson in the first place: to find out how complicit the two of them were in bribery and corruption. If that was the case, clever Stella! She finally managed to get back at one of the men who had abused her, even if she didn't live to savour her triumph.

As I think this, I realise my feelings towards Stella have come full circle and returned to what they were before she died. OK, so she kept a lot from me. Maybe that was just as well. It would have disturbed me to know what she was planning and I certainly would have tried to dissuade her. Maybe she did take advantage of me in the past, and maybe she didn't love me as much as I loved her, but she was my closest friend and I feel I shouldn't sit in judgment on her. For me, Stella was the woman who had everything. But in the end this situation did her no favours: she had poor judgment of people and her expectation that others would always act in the way that she wanted, misfired badly and ultimately tragically.

# Epilogue

I'm rearranging my bedroom ready for the baby's imminent arrival and have already filled a cupboard with baby equipment and several drawers with "unisex" baby clothes. (I decided I didn't want to know the sex when I went for the twenty-week scan).

I put the crib JC and Sarah have given me, against the wall and unwrap the new mobile I've bought – it's a very pretty one with brightly coloured birds and butterflies. Looking for the best place to hang it, I find I'll need to move a framed photo on the wall above the crib. It's one of the photos I retrieved from Stella's flat. Taken at a pop festival on the Isle of Wight, it shows the two of us, aged about seventeen, with our arms around each other. I love the photo although it emphasises the physical contrast between us: Stella looks ravishing as usual while I resemble a sack of potatoes.

I've just dragged up a chair to climb on when the doorbell goes.

It's Robbie. He's taken to calling round after work in the evenings to see if I need help with anything. Robbie seems to have become a permanent fixture in my life. I've tried to discourage him as he's ten years younger than me, but he takes no notice and I'm resigned, no, *happy*, to have him around.

When I show him the mobile he offers to hang it for me and move the photo. He peers up at it. 'You looked …different then.'

'I'm afraid I was horizontally challenged in those days… just as I am again now!' I glance ruefully down at my distended abdomen.

'Only because of what's in there!' He lays a gentle hand on my bump. 'I think you're beautiful.'

I gaze at him in disbelief. No-one has ever said I was beautiful before.

He climbs on the chair and reaches up to grasp the photo but as he unhooks it, it slips out of the frame and falls onto the floor by my feet.

I gaze at it helplessly. 'I'm afraid I can't bend like this.'

Robbie jumps off the chair, picks up the photo and hands it to me.

As I take it from him I notice that something has been written on the reverse side. It's in Stella's handwriting and my heart leaps with joy as I read it.

*Me and Hanna, my very best friend.*

* * *

It's a long and painful birth. Maria and Robbie are with me throughout.

It's a little girl! Her eyes are dark blue and her hair is blonde, almost white. She's unbelievably beautiful and, in memory of Stella, I'm going to call her Rose.

# Also by the author

If you want to read more by V K McGivney, her debut novel, *Aftermath of a Murder*, is available from Amazon in e-book format and paperback.

Aftermath Series Book One:
## Aftermath of a Murder

A gripping psychological thriller

Why was accountant Howard Armstrong murdered when he was leaving his office one afternoon?

After her husband is gunned down by an unknown assailant, his traumatised widow, Karen, is left to bring up three children on her own. The marriage had not been happy and as the investigation into his murder gets underway, she is horrified to discover that Howard had been leading a secret life of which she was totally unaware. Each new revelation hits her like a seismic shock, but she is determined to keep her children from learning the terrible truth about their father. She takes them on a trip to Wales where she experiences a peace and sense of freedom that formerly eluded her. On their return she sinks into depression and is persuaded to join a therapy group. Here she finds a vital clue leading to the discovery of the identity of Howard's murderer.

*A great plot that leads the reader deeper and deeper into the secrets and lies on which the main character's life has been unknowingly based. A gripping read that was very hard to put down.* Amazon Customer.

*Page-turning murder mystery with a gripping plot and a heart moving family story to go with it - highly recommend and an excellent first novel.* Jules Cav.

## Inheritors of the New Kingdom

### An exciting thriller

After witnessing an extraordinary object in the sky, research student Richard Jarman learns that the greenbelt around London has been partially devastated by fire. Convinced that what he saw was responsible, he confides his suspicions to Fiona, a beautiful single mother and to an elderly nun who witnessed the same phenomenon.

As the trail of destruction spreads across the globe, Richard becomes obsessed with finding the cause. The nun disappears in mysterious circumstances and he embarks on a dangerous mission to find her. He falls into the brutal clutches of a shadowy cult whose terrifying leader, Abraham R, seems to have a connection with the spate of disasters occurring around the world.

When the planet is threatened by an even greater peril, Richard and Fiona consult a famous medium, Morgana Delph and believe they have found an explanation for what is happening. But is it the right one?

*The novel beautifully juxtaposes a so-called normal reality with other worlds that are often tangential to that normalcy. Brutalising cults, extraterrestrial invasion, mediums -- all cast a lengthening shadow over the fragile surfaces of culture and civilisation. And until almost the last page, it is unclear which of these impulses will prevail. (...) a highly inventive and engrossing piece of writing, which I can warmly recommend to any reader.* Amazon customer.

*A considered and well-paced story which evolves towards a very thought-provoking ending. If you enjoy science fiction, I can't recommend this highly enough. It's an absolute corker of a tale.* Ignite.

## A Reluctant Hero

*What can a man do when his life reaches an impasse?*

Harry Saunders is unhappily married, in a job he hates and has a Big Birthday looming.

A passionate cinephile, he uses films as an escape from dreary reality, viewing the people and situations he meets through the prism of classic movies.

Harry is resigned to a bleak future until a sudden and unpremeditated act of courage propels him into a succession of sometimes absurd, sometimes dangerous, but ultimately life-changing situations.

*Just the sort of book for a relaxing holiday. It has humour, a plot, a likeable hero and a satisfactory outcome.* Janet Mary Tomson.

*Gently paced, full of humour and pathos, the character is extremely likeable if a little hapless. I'd really recommend this as a holiday read - it passes the hours very nicely indeed.* Peagreen.

## Ghosts, Resolution and Revenge

A Collection of varied and original Short Stories.

A lost hat, a free lunch, a bullied schoolgirl, a piano that plays itself, an old man's secret, a downtrodden wife's revenge - these are some of the themes of the short stories in this rich and varied collection.

The eleven tales in the anthology employ a mixture of humour, pathos, mystery and the supernatural to present a range of intriguing and challenging human situations. Some explore the decisions made by people at crisis moments in their life; others have plot twists and turns that the reader won't see coming.

*A superb and rich collection of very short stories.* Miriam Smith.

*A fantastic selection of short stories, covering different genres of writing (...) It is a true art form to be able to leave someone feeling for the characters in such a short space of time when you don't have a whole book to set the scene.* Kelly M.

*This has all that you need for a little shiver, a little nod of recognition and a little escapism.* SkullWitchery.